"You don't need two boyfriends!"

"Mary Sue! What's the matter with you? You can't possibly believe that. I can't stand Pete Milton. If you must know, I think he's a creep."

"Thanks for telling me I have such good taste," Mary Sue said coolly. "I know who my friends are and you're not one of them, Kaite Grover." Mary Sue hung up.

Bewildered and feeling the threat of tears, I raced upstairs. What had happened? I'd started out to do a favor for a friend, but got kissed by a boy I didn't like and Mark saw it. Now Mark and Mary Sue are angry with me.

"It's not my fault!"

Caprice Romances from Tempo Books

A CAPRICE ROMANCE

Ready, Set, Love

Judith Enderle

TEMPO BOOKS, NEW YORK

For the girl in Torrance who asked why no one ever wrote a story about a big family.

READY, SET, LOVE

A Tempo Book/published by arrangement with
the author

PRINTING HISTORY
Tempo Original/May 1985

ISBN: 0-441-70834-X

Chapter One

KAITE SEARCHED THROUGH her dresser drawers. She looked on her bedside table and even under her bed. She looked in the bathroom and all through her purse.

"All right!" she shouted. "Who's got it?"

"Who's got what?" Mom poked her head around the door frame. Her arms were wrapped around a pile of towels, all neatly folded and stacked as high as her chin.

For a minute Kaite felt guilty. Earlier, she'd promised to help Mom with the laundry.

"My brand-new blue eye shadow, Mom. I've only used it twice. It was right here on my side of the dresser." Kaite said *my side* because the other side belonged to her younger sister Lissa.

"Ask around," Mom said.

"But, Mom . . ."

"When you find the culprit, Kaite, I'll say and do what's necessary. But I haven't time to look right now. PB is napping, and I have to take these few minutes to get other things done."

"I said I'd help," Kaite said defensively.

Mom sighed. "Just find out what the kids are up to." She faded back into the shadows of the upstairs hall.

I'll find out what the kids are up to, all right, Kaite thought. And when I find out who took my eye shadow . . .

The most likely culprits were the twins. Every big family probably had one set. The Grovers had Eddie and Eric. They were eight years old and a force unto themselves. Usually aiding and abetting them was ten-year-old Jason. Lissa, who shared Kaite's room, was twelve, but she didn't care about makeup yet—just books; she read everything printed, even cereal boxes and directions for how to do things.

That was five kids including Kaite, which usually sounded like a lot to most people, but there were two more. At two years old, PB was the baby of the family. PB stood for Pooh Bear, which was what the Grovers called Robert because he was still a cuddly and carefree spirit. Between PB and the twins came Betsy who was six. She was the dress-up princess and another prime candidate for culprit where Kaite's eye shadow was concerned.

Kaite went to her bedroom window and pushed aside the lacy priscillas. Jason and the twins were playing some kind of game on the back lawn. It looked as if Jason was losing, since he was on the bottom of the pile.

Lissa was reading a book in the fall-apart lounge under the old oak at the back of the yard. The Grovers called the old redwood lounge the fall-apart lounge ever since Dad sat in it and it fell apart. He'd put some new bolts in the wood and painted the lounge bright yellow, but it was still the fall-apart lounge to the family.

Kaite had ruled out PB as the eye shadow thief. If he'd been into her eye shadow, Mom would have known about it because he would have had a case of blue mouth. PB tasted everything. Mom had gone to the hospital with him twice because of it. Fortunately Dad was on staff there, and so the doctors and nurses knew everyone in the Grover family.

Betsy was nowhere in sight. She might be on the front lawn playing with her dolls. She liked to spread a blanket and pretend that it was her house. She usually tried to stay clear of Jason and the twins who always wanted to play Giant and trample her and her family.

From the upstairs window, Kaite couldn't spot the guilty party. She hurried down the steps, around the corner, through the kitchen, and out into the yard.

"We've captured the invader," Eddie shouted. "Take him to our spaceship."

"I'm not the invader if you have the spaceship," Jason said, as he wiggled out from under them. "You two are the invaders. Remember?" He pushed them aside. From the expression on his face, Kaite knew he'd seen her coming. "Uh-oh. Enemy sighted at the back door, you guys. Head for the escape hatch."

As Eddie and Eric struggled to their feet, Kaite saw what had happened to her eye shadow. They had blue streaks all over their faces, blue stars on the back of each hand, and blue down the fronts of their shirts.

"We didn't use all of it, Kaite. There's some left," Eric shouted as they raced for the side of the house.

Forgetting that she'd just turned *sweet* sixteen, she took off after them. "I'll kill you brats," she shouted, as she leaped over the wagon and dodged a football in her path. She must have sounded as if she meant it—and for a minute she did—because they had disappeared by the time Kaite reached the front yard. Betsy was the only one in sight. She was on the porch with her friend Amy. They were playing with trucks today instead of playing house.

"Where did they go?" Kaite yelled. Amy pointed

down the street, but Kaite didn't see any one of the three. "They'll be sorry." With hands on her hips, she carefully scanned every possible hiding place for signs of her brothers. But wherever they were, they didn't give a clue to their presence. "I'll be waiting," she shouted, and turned toward the door.

Back inside, Kaite stopped in the kitchen to get a glass of orange juice. Leaning against the pine cabinets, she stared at the refrigerator plastered with original Grover family art, mostly the twins' and Betsy's contributions. It had been a long time since one of Kaite's masterpieces had hung in the kitchen gallery.

Being the oldest is getting to be a royal pain in the kazoo, she thought. I always have to help with the work, while the kids get away with murder. One of these days I'll go on strike. Meanwhile, she wondered where the twins had put what was left of her eye shadow.

She rinsed her glass and intercepted Mom on her way back into the kitchen. PB was snuggled in her arms. A red streak ran down the side of his face where he'd pressed against the wrinkles in his sheets. His thumb was poked firmly into his mouth. "Hi, Pooh," Kaite said, and ruffled his fine blond hair.

He snuggled closer to Mom, giving his thumb a real good workout.

People always said they'd know a Grover kid anywhere. They all had blue eyes, blond hair, and were skinny. It wasn't that they didn't eat, they were just skinny—even Mom and Dad.

"Did you find your eye shadow?" Mom said, crossing Laundry off her list on the bulletin board.

"The twins *borrowed* it. They're playing Outer Space."

Mom nodded. "I'll take care of it. Meanwhile, Kaite, would you switch the sheets into the dryer and put the dark clothes into the washer? That will finish all the laundry for today.''

"Sure, Mom." Kaite stepped into the laundry room, which was right off the kitchen. While she sorted the dark clothes, checking pockets and looking for rips and missing buttons, she thought of a dozen tortures for Eddie and Eric. Nothing Mom could say or do would make up for the loss of her new eye shadow. And she probably wouldn't even get it replaced. Money for extras wasn't easy to come by in their family. Even though her father was a doctor, he didn't roll in green paper, as he always said. And Kaite was so busy helping and baby-sitting at home for free, she rarely had time to get an outside job. Not fair! she thought.

Her friend Mary Sue Cariatti was so lucky. There were only three kids in her family. Her older brother Dennis was almost never around because he went to college as well as working part-time at the market. Then there was her little sister Tricia, but she wasn't the pest Kaite's brothers and sisters were.

The other way Mary Sue was lucky was that she had a figure. Kaite was trying to be resigned to never having one. Sixteen already and still flat as a board. Well, she did have some ridges. But if you're not a Ruffles potato chip, ridges aren't enough. You want the real thing. Mom always said not to worry. "Time will take care of your figure," she'd say. She didn't have to worry. She had a nice figure. Everyone asked her how she could have all those kids and be so slim. She said it was because of all those kids she stayed that way. No time to sit down, she always said.

Kaite heard giggling, then the back door slammed. "Eric, Eddie, is that you?" She tried to sound patient and sweet and understanding, like Mom. No answer. She knew it was them. What were they up to now?

She pulled out the knob on the washer to make the water flow in, measured some soap powder, and banged the lid shut on the machine. Closing the laundry room door against the steady hum of the dryer and the impending chunk-a-chunk of the washer, she tiptoed toward the kitchen window. Only Lissa was still in back. She hurried through the house toward the front. No sign of anyone now. It was almost too quiet. More than once Mom had said that quiet around the house was ominous—a sure sign of trouble coming.

Kaite opened the front door and stepped onto the porch. Amy's and Betsy's trucks were still lined up across the cement. Then she noticed a pile of leaves and debris in the center of the sidewalk. It must have come from the two big myoporum bushes that grew at the edge of the property and from the little jacaranda tree Mom was nursing on the parking strip in hopes of seeing blue flowers, she thought. Sometimes Mom even talked to that tree. But what was the mess doing on the sidewalk? Kaite wondered. The wind, which could suddenly whip up from the desert, was calm today. And this was spring, not fall, when some trees shed their leaves.

Frowning and suspicious, Kaite stepped over the trucks and started down the walk. She stopped as she caught a glimpse of a marvelous sight down the block and heading her way. She smoothed her thin blond hair and hoped it wasn't too messy. How she wished she had her blue eye shadow on right then. I'll send those kids to the moon! she thought. Self-consciously she smoothed her T-shirt down over the waistband of her faded jeans. Ready, Kaite, she thought, as she watched the long, easy strides of Mark O'Connell, West Valley High's track star.

Mark could outrun them all. He was tall like Kaite's dad; he had blue eyes, too, but his hair was shiny black and curly. Kaite's heart thumped in time to his footsteps. Should I sit on the steps or keep standing? she wondered, as he came closer.

He wore black nylon running shorts and a white shirt was tied around his waist. His face, chest, and shoulders were shiny with sweat. He must have been running a long way, she thought.

She backed toward the porch, almost tripped over one of the trucks, then changed her mind. What if he thinks the trucks are mine? A stupid thought, she decided. Why would he think that? Because you look so young, so flat, so average. If I had to be born first in this family, why couldn't I at least have been born beautiful? Kaite asked herself.

There was nothing she could do about her looks at that moment, but she could say something to Mark. "Hi," she whispered, practicing. "Hi, Mark." Something seemed to be wrong with her voice. If she talked out loud, Kaite was sure she'd squeak or something worse. She glanced down the street. He was only two houses away.

She moved away from the porch. A chance like this comes once in a girl's lifetime. In her imagination, he was slowing his stride. He was stopping. He was asking her—Kaite Grover—for a date. Please, she thought, at least make him look at me.

When she glanced up, he was in front of her house at the end of the walk. He looked right at her and smiled. Stunned that her prayer really had been answered, Kaite smiled back and jammed her hands into her pockets and said—nothing. In a minute he'd be gone, a blur down the street. But he was slowing down, and he glanced back over his shoulder at her. Kaite started to say hi, when everything, including Mark O'Connell, suddenly went topsy-turvy.

Giggles came from the myoporum bushes. The pile of leaves flew into the air. And Mark O'Connell sprawled in the center of the sidewalk.

"We captured one!" Eric emerged from the dense cover of the bushes.

"Oh, no! What did you kids do?" Kaite ran toward Mark, who was lying on his side clutching his ankle. He closed his eyes and seemed very still as she approached.

Eddie, Eric, Jason, Betsy, and Amy gathered around him.

"Geez, we didn't mean for you to get hurt," Eddie said.

Kaite stared down at Mark. For a minute, she felt frozen. Not even her voice worked.

"Kaite, maybe you should get Mom." Jason's voice sounded little and scared.

"Are you dead?" Betsy touched him with her foot.

"Don't be silly," Kaite snapped, pulling her back. But he was very still. "You aren't dead, are you? I didn't take CPR yet," she babbled.

Mark opened his eyes and looked directly at her. "CPR is no good on ankles." He tried to smile, but instead a grimace spread across his face.

"Do you need help?" Kaite knelt down beside him, hoping that he'd stand up and at least limp away. Behind her the kids watched solemnly. Now she saw what had happened. They'd stretched the old volleyball net across the sidewalk and concealed it with leaves. One end was tied to the base of the jacaranda tree; the other end had been held by one of them in the clump of bushes. Before Mark stepped on the net, they'd tugged and tripped him up. What a dumb stunt! Really dangerous!

Mark gripped his ankle. "I'm still alive, I think, but I could have used a warning." His jaw tightened and he inhaled sharply.

"I—I'm sorry. I didn't know they were—" Kaite's face felt warm as he looked at her. Doesn't he believe me? she wondered. She jumped up and raced for the house. "I'll get my mother."

"Hurry," Eric called.

"I'll murder them. I'll be an only child before this day is through," she muttered. How could they? Wait until Mark told everyone at school—especially about the CPR. She'd be the laughingstock of West Valley High. She banged the door open. "Mom, come quick!"

"What's wrong, Kaite?" Mom called over the upstairs railing.

"The kids booby-trapped the sidewalk in front and someone got hurt."

"Oh, my gosh! What next?" Mom raced down the stairs with PB tucked under one arm. "Take the baby. Who's hurt? How badly?"

"His name is Mark O'Connell. He's the captain of the track team at school." As soon as Kaite said those words she knew that things weren't just bad; they were, as Betsy would say, the worstest.

"Kaite, is he seriously hurt? Do I need the first-aid kit? Should I call your father?"

Kaite stared into her mother's patient blue eyes. "I don't know. I don't know anything, Mom." With PB tucked under her arm, she ran upstairs, leaving her mother to take care of Mark and everything else. She couldn't face him. She just couldn't!

Chapter Two

"A SPRAINED ANKLE," Dad said as they sat down to the dinner table. He looked solemn and when he stared at Jason and the twins, they looked down at their plates.

Kaite couldn't remember Dad yelling as loudly or as long as he did when he came home.

"Will Mark be able to run?" she asked, fearing what the answer would be.

"Not tomorrow," Dad said curtly. He passed the bowl of mashed potatoes to Jason, who took only a little of his favorite food and passed them on.

The dinner table hadn't been as subdued as it was that night for a long time. Everyone was in trouble, even Kaite for running upstairs instead of helping Mom with Mark. She'd tried to explain how embarrassed she'd felt, but her parents wouldn't listen to any excuses. She still didn't know how Mom managed to get Mark to the car and didn't have enough nerve to ask. The only good thing that had happened was that her eye shadow had been returned, what was left of it. Eddie'd had it in his pocket.

All day Sunday, even during church services, Kaite thought about what would happen when she went to school. Maybe Mark wouldn't be there and no one would find out right away. If only she could be that lucky! Several times she reached for the phone to call Mary Sue, but each time changed her mind. Kaite didn't want anyone to know what had happened, not even her best friend.

On Monday, she was tempted to tell Mom that she didn't feel well, but one look at her mother's face, and Kaite knew she was waiting for her excuse. She skipped breakfast and dragged her feet all the way to the bus stop.

Mary Sue was waiting, all enthusiastic about the new outfit her mom bought for her over the weekend.

"Yeah. It's real cute," Kaite said, noticing the peach-striped pants and top her friend was wearing.

"And guess what else? My mom said I could get a perm this summer." Mary Sue fluffed her straight, silky dark hair. "Did you hear me?" She poked Kaite with her elbow.

Kaite moved away and frowned.

"What's the matter with you?"

"You don't know what happened to me." *If we could just have an earthquake now, not too big, but big enough to stop the bus from coming, big enough to close school for a while,* she prayed. But earthquakes couldn't be wished or prayed for, she guessed. The only shaking Kaite felt was Mary Sue shaking her.

"Are you grounded or something?" she asked.

"I wish I were, permanently, every hour of every day. It would be better than this, believe me."

Mary Sue's dark brown eyes opened wide. "What happened?"

"I'll tell you in a minute."

The bus brakes hissed as the huge yellow and white vehicle eased to a stop in front of them. Kaite followed Mary Sue to a center seat and watched as about ten other kids clambered aboard behind them. The doors flapped shut and the driver accelerated into traffic on Ventura Boulevard.

"So, what happened to make you sound as if you'd like to be martyred?" Mary Sue asked.

"Mark O'Connell happened."

"*The* Mark O'Connell from school?" Mary Sue's voice rose with excitement.

Kaite nodded. "The *lame* Mark O'Connell."

"We're not talking about the same guy. I mean the track star: tall, blue eyes that could make you cry, with long thick lashes to make you jealous, and those black curls." Mary Sue sighed. "Why did you even bring up his name, Kaite?"

"Because you asked me, and because—because of him, I'm going to be the laughingstock of the entire West Valley High School, not to mention being on everyone's villain of the year list. What's a lady villain called, anyway?"

"A villainess?" Mary Sue wrinkled her nose and giggled. "I don't know. You've got to tell me the whole story. Start from the beginning."

Kaite began with the eye shadow.

"What an opportunity!" Mary Sue shook her head and slid down in the seat as Kaite finished. "Nothing like that ever happens to me."

"And my brothers and sisters ruined it for me." Kaite still felt the urge to kill, maim, strangle, and do definite bodily harm. Lucky for her brothers she was basically a peaceful person.

"Maybe not. Maybe Mark's the forgiving type."

Kaite stared at her friend. "Mary Sue, why should he be? He won't be able to run until his ankle heals. If you were captain of the track team, the star, would you be forgiving?"

Mary Sue didn't answer. She sat up straight and poked Kaite. "Look who's lowered himself to take the bus."

Distracted for the moment from her own problems, Kaite glanced toward the front of the bus. Pete Milton, Mr. Ego himself, stood surveying the choice of seats.

"Probably trying to decide who gets the honor of his company," Mary Sue said.

"Just because he turned you down for the Turnabout Dance doesn't mean . . . ." Kaite began.

"Don't defend him," Mary Sue interrupted. "You defend everyone. You know I'm right. Look at his perfect jeans, his perfect brown hair, his perfect white shirt. Look at him swaggering this way. Just look at him. An opportunity—" Mary Sue mumbled the rest of her sentence, and Kaite wondered if her friend knew that she'd sighed out loud.

She was right about one thing. Pete's attitude was: I'm important—just ask me.

He stopped beside them and dropped casually into the seat across the aisle. "Hi, Kaite." He winked and smiled at her.

"Hi," she answered. He was cute—not as cute as . . . . Forget Mark! she told herself.

Mary Sue slid down in the seat again. Kaite could feel her friend's agony. Mary Sue'd been trying to get him to notice her since September.

"Did you have a nice weekend, Kaite?" Pete leaned his arm on the seat in front of him. The man sitting there turned around, but Pete didn't pay attention. "My dad let me take his new Jeep for a drive. I *could* come by and take you for a ride this afternoon.'' He winked and grinned.

What was that supposed to mean? Kaite wondered. She glanced at Mary Sue, whose mouth had dropped open, then she looked back at Pete. This had to be a joke. He'd never glanced her way before now. She smiled. "Nice of you to ask, but I don't think I can. My dad's kind of strict about the kind of cars I ride in.'' She felt stupid. That sounded as if she were a baby in elementary school. And anyway, there was nothing wrong with Jeeps. Why didn't I just say no thanks? she wondered.

Pete shrugged. He ran a hand through his sun-streaked brown hair. "If you change your mind, let me know.'' He got up and walked down the aisle where he sat beside Josie Cameron.

"Fat chance,'' Mary Sue muttered.

Kaite turned around and glanced at Pete. Would he be so bad to go out with? Glancing at her friend, Kaite knew that despite her sarcastic words she was thinking the same thing.

The bus stopped with a jolt in front of school. Everyone pushed toward the bus doors. Not many other people except students rode this early run. Kaite guessed that most waited for the next bus. Some people were very anti-kid.

Kaite jumped from the bus step to the grass and followed Mary Sue toward the walk.

"Don't forget; my offer still stands.'' Pete tapped her shoulder lightly as he passed them on the steps.

Mary Sue imitated him as they walked down the hall. Her pride had really been wounded in February. But Kaite knew she still liked him.

"Never mind him.'' Kaite looked nervously down the length of the hall. "What am I going to do if Mark shows up at school today? What if he tells everyone what happened and what I said about CPR? I'll just die.''

"You won't die, and anyway you probably won't even see him if he does come to school. He's a senior, remember?''

"I remember everything.'' Kaite turned toward her locker and spun the combination, missing twice before the lock opened. Her books were heaped on the floor, and she poked through them, searching for those she'd need that morning. "Mary Sue, did you do the history assignment?''

Mary Sue didn't answer.

"Mary Sue?'' Kaite glanced sideways and gulped. Her eyes traveled up the length of a metal crutch right to the serious face and blue eyes of Mark O'Connell. She stood up quickly, forgetting that she'd been piling books on her lap. They tumbled in a mass at her feet.

Mark quickly hopped backward as her history book just missed his toes. "Kaite? Um, Kaite Grover?''

Feeling stupid, she nodded.

"I was wondering—'' He hesitated. "May I have your phone number?''

Any other time she'd have danced a jig down the center of the hall. But at the moment, her mind went blank and she couldn't even remember if they had any telephones at her house, let alone what the number was.

"It's 555-2960,'' Mary Sue said, answering for her.

"Thanks. Is it okay if I call you, Kaite?''

His eyes look so blue, she thought. "Call me? Yes. Sure. I mean, okay.'' Kaite bit her lip to keep from asking when—or why. She looked at the floor and grabbed one of the books she'd dropped. The quiz papers she kept inside the cover fanned out at her feet. This was terrible. She felt so clumsy. Why was she such a bumbler when Mark was around? He must think

. . . well, she didn't want to know what he must think by now.

"I wish I could help you pick up your books, but . . ." Mark glanced at his ankle.

"I can do it." She pulled the books toward her into a sloppy pile.

Mark sighed. "I'll be calling you. Okay?" He turned away. "Oh, I almost forgot. Give this to your mom, please." He reached into his jacket pocket and handed her an envelope. What was in it? she wondered. Maybe it was a letter from his attorney. Maybe he was going to sue them?

"How's—how's your ankle?" she asked. "Does it hurt a lot?"

"Not too much now." He glanced down. "But it's definitely sprained." He smiled. "CPR might have been interesting, but it wouldn't have helped."

He remembered! Kaite busily gathered up the rest of her books, afraid to look up to see if he looked teasing or serious. "I'm sorry that you got hurt," she said, smoothing the cover of her English book.

"Me, too."

The tone of his voice made Kaite look up again, and her heart did somersaults when he smiled. She felt like crying. If only those kids . . .

"Hey, Mark, what happened to you?" A couple of his friends came down the hall and he turned toward them.

"Hi, Brian, Chris," he called. They walked slowly away as the bell shrilled the warning for the start of classes. Kaite couldn't hear what he said, but they turned around and looked at her.

Please, she prayed, about that earthquake. Now would be a good time. Kaite was ready for the big one to swallow her up right then and there. Anything would be better.

"He's so cute," Mary Sue said.

Kaite was startled by her friend's words. She'd forgotten Mary Sue was there.

"Maybe this will turn out all right after all." Mary Sue leaned against the next locker and sighed.

"Oh, sure, and maybe I'm going to get an A in biology, too," Kaite said. "Miracles don't happen. Of that I'm sure. I've prayed for enough of them." She wondered if she should count the prayer she'd said just before Mark was tripped. If that was an answer to her prayer, she thought she'd better be very careful what she prayed for. "More likely he's going to take us to court."

"Is that what your dad expects?"

"I don't know and I don't dare ask." Kaite had a sinking feeling in the pit of her stomach. The whole family would be grounded forever if that happened, right down to PB. Dad put up with a lot, but he wouldn't like going to court. If the kids thought he yelled this weekend, she had a feeling they hadn't heard a whisper yet. "Let's go somewhere after school." Kaite stuck the envelope Mark gave her in her purse, then gathered her books back into a pile on the floor. "I don't want to be home when Mark calls."

"What! You're crazy." Mary Sue went to her locker, which was a few down from Kaite's.

"I'm not, either. I'll call Mom and tell her I'm going to the Mall with you. You call your mom and do the same. Then that's where we'll go."

"I don't think I can."

"Please, Mary Sue."

"I'll call and ask. But I can't promise." She slammed her locker door.

"You can talk your mom into anything."

"Wrong."

"Try. It's important."

The final bell rang before Kaite could argue with her

anymore. They scooped up their books and hurried. She couldn't be late for English. Mrs. Miles believed in assigning essays to anyone who was late. And she always chose the weirdest topics, like, "How to Defend the Albino Dodo Bird Against the Ravages of Extinction by the Cave Man."

Out of breath when she reached English class, Kaite dropped into her seat, which happened to be in front of Jay Harrisman. "Hey, Kaite," he whispered, "I hear you did in our track star this weekend. If I were you, I'd avoid Coach Evans."

Kaite couldn't even defend herself. She just slumped down in the seat and expected that her whole day was going to be like that.

Mary Sue's mom said she could go to the Mall, but only for an hour. Kaite's mom wasn't too thrilled about the idea, either, but Kaite begged to be allowed to go.

"From now on, Kaite," her mom said, "I have to know your plans before you go to school. I have to buy shoes for the twins today. Now I have to take Betsy and PB with me." PB could destroy a store in only a few minutes. He was interested in everything.

Kaite bit her tongue to keep from saying anything to make her mother angry. Kaite, the maid. Kaite, the built-in baby-sitter. Kaite, the bad-luck kid, she thought. She seemed to fit all three descriptions, and she didn't like any of them.

Although it was being remodeled and expanded, the Victory Mall already had dozens of stores. Kaite and Mary Sue wandered around the scaffoldings and through the best clothing stores although neither of them had money to buy anything. Kaite saw so many cute clothes she'd love to have, she could hardly stand it. Maybe coming here wasn't such a good idea at that, she thought as they passed a display of white cotton jumpsuits that made her want to pray for yet another miracle. They hurried on to the next place.

They stayed clear of the shoe store, however. Kaite was afraid she'd run into her mom, who'd ask Mary Sue what she'd bought since that was the excuse Kaite'd given her. Too soon, their hour was up and it was time to catch the bus home.

"Call me later," Mary Sue called as they parted at the corner.

"I'll try."

Lissa was sitting on the porch reading *Watership Down* when Kaite turned up the walk.

"Jason, she's home," Lissa called, loud enough for the whole block to hear.

Jason yanked open the front door. Behind him the phone shrilled. "Hurry, Kaite. It's probably him again."

This was the first time she'd seen Jason harried.

"You answer it. I'm not home." She pushed past him.

Jason grabbed her arm. "Yes, you are. I'm tired of answering the phone." He stomped toward the kitchen and then the phone stopped ringing. "She's finally here." He poked his head around the kitchen door frame and held out the receiver.

Kaite sighed and took it. "Hello?" Her voice didn't sound like her own at all.

"Hello, Kaite. This is Mark O'Connell, the victim."

She swallowed. "Um, hi."

"Are you busy this Friday?"

"Um, no," she replied cautiously.

"Good. Will you go to the movies with me?"

"The movies?" Not to court?

"There are a lot of good movies playing. We can decide during the week which one we want to see—if you'll go with me, that is."

"Sure. I'd love to." Kaite's voice sounded stronger and her heart was beating a hundred miles an hour. It's a good thing my wish for the earthquake didn't come true, she thought. She guessed she'd better be more careful about what she wished for.

"See you at school tomorrow. Oh, and did you give your mom the envelope?"

"Not yet. I just got home." And she'd completely forgotten about the envelope.

"Oh. Well, don't forget. Okay?"

Kaite nodded, then realized he couldn't see her. "I won't."

"See you then. Bye." He hung up and so did she.

Was he out for revenge? Was that why he asked me out? Kaite wondered. Quickly she dialed Mary Sue's number.

Chapter
Three

"KAITE, ARE YOU HOME?" Mom's voice called out over PB's whining while the twins shouted, "Look at my new shoes." Betsy paraded past wearing Mom's straw garden hat.

"I have to go, Mary Sue. See you tomorrow."

"Okay. And stop worrying."

"Easy for you to say. Bye." Kaite hung up and went to see what her mother wanted.

"Would you please carry in the grocery bags for me? I stopped on the way home and picked up some frozen pizza and a few other things. I don't have the time or energy to fix dinner tonight." Mom did look exhausted as she pried PB loose from her neck and put him on a chair, where he immediately demanded that she pick him up again.

"Be quiet, PB," Kaite said. "Go find Lissa." Where was her sister, anyway? Obviously not in front any longer, or she'd be carrying in groceries. Probably hiding out somewhere with her book. Kaite jumped down off the back porch, dodged Amy, who seemed to have a special sense about when Betsy was home, and went to the station wagon parked in the drive. There were four bags of groceries. She grabbed two, carried them inside, and ran back for the other two. Together she and her mother unpacked the bags in the kitchen.

"Thanks for the help, Kaite. Did you see Mark O'Connell at school?" Mom asked, as she closed the refrigerator.

"He came by my locker this morning and—I almost forgot! He gave me something for you."

Kaite grabbed her purse from the floor where she'd dropped it with her books when she'd answered the phone. After all the trouble of going to the Mall, she hadn't been able to avoid his phone call and was still uncertain about the reasons he was asking her out.

"Mark said to give you this, Mom." Kaite handed her the envelope, slightly bent at the corners from being jammed in her purse.

Mom slit open the flap and pulled out a card. "How nice. A thank you note," she said, handing it to Kaite. "There's a boy with nice manners."

"He asked me to go to a movie with him this Friday."

"Friday?" Mom frowned. "Your father and I have a Medical Association dinner that evening, Kaite, and . . ."

Kaite barely kept herself from stamping her feet. Instead she clenched her fists. "Mom! It's not fair. When do I get to have a life of my own? Can't Lissa watch the kids just this once? She's old enough. Anyway, I told Mark I'd love to go to the movies." She struggled to keep her voice low, but she still sounded as if she was shouting.

Mom stared at her. "I didn't know I was imposing on you, Kaite," she said in an even but angry voice.

Kaite took a deep breath. "Sometimes you are, Mom. It seems as if I have to live my life around Lissa,

Jason, Eric, Eddie, Betsy, and PB. Lissa hides in her books. And the others are too little to worry about anything but themselves. It seems as if I always have to help, always be the one in charge when you're not here, always keep track of where the kids are. I need time for me, Mom. Please?''

"In a large family, everyone has to have some duties, Kaite Elizabeth.'' Her mother folded the grocery bags and put them in the pantry.

Mom had called her Kaite Elizabeth, which meant she was pretty annoyed. "I know, Mom. But sometimes it seems as if I have them all. Why can't you give the others some duties?''

Why had she started this conversation? Now Mom probably would say she definitely couldn't go anywhere with Mark. Most likely she'd just gotten herself grounded.

Mom stared at Kaite for a minute, then nodded. "Let me discuss this with your father.''

"You mean, I can go out Friday?'' Kaite's voice rose again, this time with excitement.

"I mean, I'll discuss it with your father,'' her mother said evenly.

PB toddled into the kitchen. He wrapped his arms around Mom's legs. "PB stinky,'' he said.

Mom looked at her. "Kaite,'' she began. Then she stopped. "Come on, PB.'' Mom took his hand and they left the kitchen.

"Hey, Kaite, where's Mom?'' Lissa, a notebook tucked under her arm, leaned around the kitchen door.

"In the bathroom with PB. Where have you been?''

"Upstairs studying. Will you tell Mom I had to go to the library? I need more books for my term paper.''

"It's your night to set the table.''

"I'll be back in time. If I'm not, Jason can do it. Or you can do it.''

"I have homework, too,'' Kaite shouted as her sister

headed for the door. "And if you expect Jason to do your job, you'd better tell him."

Lissa slammed the front door.

Kaite ran upstairs to her room. Friday just had to be all right. If Dad said she couldn't go, she'd just die. In fact, she'd die twice—once because she couldn't go and the other time because she'd have to tell Mark she couldn't go.

Kaite flopped on her bed and pictured how he looked. Even if he asked her out for some kind of revenge, it was still a date. Mary Sue was right. It was stupid to worry about ulterior motives.

Lissa didn't get back in time to set the table, and Jason said it wasn't his night. So naturally Kaite set the table. Kaite didn't think Mom noticed but she decided not to complain. After all, Kaite'd already told her exactly how she felt about all the work she had to do.

"Kaite," said Dad when they'd finished eating, "I'd like to talk with you in my study."

The rest of the kids looked at Kaite. Only Eddie had nerve enough to say, "What did she do?"

"Help your mother clear the table," Dad said to him. He pushed his chair back and motioned to Kaite to follow him.

"And Lissa is going to put the dishes in the dishwasher," said Mom, "since she missed setting the table."

"But that's Jason's job tonight," Lissa said.

"Jason has wastepaper baskets to empty, and he has trash cans to take out," said Mom.

"But I don't know how to take out the trash cans," said Jason. "Dad always does that."

"Time you learned, son," Dad said. "That's your job from now on."

"Do I get to do jobs, too?" Betsy asked.

"You can sort the silverware from the dishwasher basket," Mom said. "And, Eddie and Eric, don't sneak off. When the dishes are cleared, Eddie cleans the sink and Eric sweeps the floor."

"How come all of a sudden we have to do all this stuff? Kaite and Lissa are supposed to do everything," Eric complained.

"Kaite and Lissa don't have as much time as they used to, and you are all able to help. We're having a little reorganization in this family," said Dad.

Kaite was glad to hear about the reorganization, but couldn't help wondering if she was in trouble, too. Maybe Dad was angry because she'd complained to Mom. Usually he didn't call them into his study unless they were in trouble. She glanced at Mom to see if she could tell from the expression on her mother's face, if she should expect the worst. But Mom was busy cleaning banana pudding off PB.

Everyone was in motion, so Kaite got up and followed Dad. His study was lined with bookshelves. Magazines and files were stacked on the corners of his desk. She felt like one of his patients as she sat in the leather armchair and he sat in his swivel desk chair. He touched his fingertips together and gave her his direct look.

"Your mother tells me you aren't happy with your responsibilities in this family, Kaite." He took off his glasses and rubbed the bridge of his nose, then put them back on.

Struggling to remain calm and feeling a bit squirmy, Kaite told her dad how she felt about being responsible for her brothers and sisters all the time.

"All the time is a bit of an exaggeration," he said. "And, as you noticed tonight, your mother and I don't entirely disagree with you. Perhaps we've tended to place the burden of your brothers and sisters on your shoulders because we know from experience that we can count on you, Kaite. Fair is fair, however, and so we're making some adjustments in the lists of respon-

sibilities around here. That doesn't mean that you don't
have to help any longer. Many times we'll expect you
to stay home and be in charge. However, Lissa and
Jason are mature enough to be dependable in some
short-term situations.''

"What about Friday?" Kaite asked. She crossed her
fingers in her lap.

"Friday?"

"Didn't Mom tell you? Mark O'Connell asked me
to go to a movie and I said I would, but she said you
have a Medical Association dinner and . . .''

Dad put up his hand to interrupt her. "You still have
to ask your mother or myself before you accept a date,
Kaite."

Everything seemed to sink inside her. "But I . . ."
His look made her stop.

"This one time we'll make an exception. However,
you must be home no later than eleven, because Lissa
has to be in bed by that time and your mother and I
won't be back until after midnight. Is that clear?"

"Oh, yes. Absolutely! Thanks, Dad." She jumped
up and ran around the desk to hug him. "No more
complaining. Ever! I promise."

Dad ruffled her hair. "Don't make promises you
can't keep, kiddo."

Kaite laughed and hugged him again. "I'll see if
Mom needs any more help in the kitchen. Thanks,
thanks, thanks."

Just then the phone rang and her father answered. It
was the hospital calling, so she slipped out of the room
and hurried to the kitchen. For someone who might be
walking right into a huge plot for revenge, I'm sure
going cheerfully, she thought.

The next morning, Kaite told Mary Sue the whole
story.

"I wish I could get my brother and sister to do more at home," her friend said.

"But Dennis is away all day and Tricia is little."

"Not that little. And my brother gets home in time to eat."

"Tell your mother. That's what worked for me— talking about it."

"I think I'll try. So, which movie are you going to see?"

"I don't know. Mark said we'd decide during the week."

"It really doesn't matter, does it?" Mary Sue sat sideways in the bus seat and stared at her.

"I don't know what you mean." Kaite knew she was blushing.

Mary Sue laughed. "Yes, you do."

Kaite poked her in the ribs, and her friend made a face as she grabbed her side.

At school, Kaite didn't see Mark at all—not in the morning and not in the afternoon. But she did see Pete Milton.

"Kaite, how about going out with me Friday night?" He lounged against the locker next to hers and grinned down at her as she struggled to sort out the books she'd need for homework. "I can get the Jeep."

"Sorry, I'm busy," Kaite said.

"Likely excuse. Probably washing your hair or visiting your grandmother. Then there's the my-cousin-is-coming-over excuse and the baby-sitting excuse. Well, I won't give up. There's always the Friday after that and the one after that. Then there are always Saturdays. Are you busy Saturday?"

"No, but . . ."

"That's all right, because I am." He laughed and walked away.

"You're not funny," Kaite muttered. And maybe

Mark O'Connell wasn't either. Was he planning to take her out once and then avoid her to get revenge? She hoped he understood that she hadn't meant for her family to cripple him. After all, it wasn't her fault that she lived in a zoo and that's how it felt a lot of times at the Grover house.

"Call me," Mary Sue said when Kaite got off the bus.

"I will." She walked slowly today, wondering where Mark had been all day. Maybe gangrene had set in, she thought. Could you get that from a sprained ankle? For a doctor's kid, she didn't know much about medicine.

The house was strangely quiet when Kaite entered, but the smell of spaghetti sauce made her stomach grumble hungrily. A note was wedged in the refrigerator door. Mom knew where all the kids headed as soon as they came home.

> Dear Kaite,
>   I've gone to a PTA planning meeting at Cabrillo Elementary, and I have a few stops to make afterward. Please stir the spaghetti sauce and remind Lissa to set the table. The rest of the kids are with me. See you around five.
>
>   Mom

Where was Lissa? Kaite wondered. Her sister should be home. She ate a container of yogurt, then went upstairs. Lissa was stretched across her bed with a book.

"Mom says not to forget to set the table."

Lissa waved a hand. Kaite guessed that meant she heard.

She changed into old jeans and a purple sweatshirt, then went back downstairs to call Mary Sue. They were still talking—once they had talked for three and a half hours—when Mom came home. Kaite was just telling Mary Sue how darling she thought Mark was—for the hundredth time—when Jason peeked around the corner.

"Oh, Mary Sue, Mark is so wonderful," he said in a squeaky voice. "I hope he'll kiss me."

"Mary Sue, hold on a minute. Jason, shut up!" Kaite yelled.

Jason laughed and ran. What a brat!

Lissa came clattering down the stairs with a paperback in her hand. "I know," she said as Mom met her at the kitchen door. "I have to set the table."

"Kaite, get off that phone," Mom ordered. "Didn't you read my note?"

"Have to go, Mary Sue. See you in the morning." She hung up. "Of course I did. I stirred the spaghetti sauce and reminded Lissa about setting the table."

"I never heard her, Mom," Lissa said.

"You did, too. You waved your arm at me. And if you never heard, how come you're here now telling Mom that you know what you have to do?" Kaite folded her arms and stared at her sister.

Lissa glared at her.

Mom sighed and grabbed a box of cookies away from Eric. "Take care of the table now, Lissa. Kaite, please change PB for me."

Lissa yanked open the silverware drawer, and Kaite scooped up her baby brother from the floor. "I wish you knew how to go potty," she said.

PB just grinned, then poked his thumb in his mouth.

After dinner the phone rang and Jason answered. "Guess who?" he called, a big grin on his face. "It's Mark; that incredible boy, Kaite."

Kaite wanted to die, but not before she strangled Jason. She grabbed the receiver from him and tried to

keep her voice calm. "Hi. Don't mind my brother.
He's practicing to be a bad comedian."

"Is he the same funny one who tripped me up with
the volleyball net?"

"One of them," Kaite admitted uncomfortably.

For a minute there was silence.

"About the movie Friday . . ." Mark began.

Had he changed his mind? Was this the revenge
part? Ask me, then drop me? she wondered.

"Is the Fallbrook Cinema okay with you? They have
a good double bill."

"Fine. Fallbrook is fine." A feeling of relief flowed
through her. "What time?"

"I'll pick you up at six-thirty."

"Oh. I have to be home by eleven—to baby-sit,"
she added.

"I think we can manage that. See you at school."

"See you." Kaite hung up.

"Does he love you?" asked Jason.

She reached for her brother but he was too quick for
her. Didn't anyone want a brother for free? Kaite had
several to give away.

Chapter Four

"GUESS WHO ASKED me for your phone number?" Mary Sue strolled beside Kaite on their way to the bus stop.

"What?"

"Quit thinking about tonight and listen." Mary Sue sounded upset.

"What's wrong?"

"Nothing is wrong. Why should something be wrong?"

"You sound mad at me."

"I never get mad at you. You're my best friend."

"What about the time I spilled chocolate syrup on your new white pants?"

"Okay. I might get a little upset once in a while. But I don't stay that way long." She really did look upset. "I'm trying to tell you something."

"Tell me what, for pity's sake?"

"I gave Pete Milton your phone number."

"*You . . . ? My* phone number?" Kaite knew her mouth was hanging open. "But why?"

"He asked me, and I didn't even stop to think, Kaite."

"But why?"

Mary Sue shrugged. "He probably wants to ask you out again."

"But why?" Kaite sounded like a broken record.

"Because he smiled at me. And don't say *but why*?"

"What I mean is, why should he want to call me or ask me out? And why did you give him my phone number, when you—"

"Who knows with Pete?" she interrupted.

"I'm not interested. Tell him that. I have."

Mary Sue's smile was sad. "Pete only listens when he wants to. And he doesn't listen when he doesn't want to, not even when he should." There was a note of hurt in her voice. She'd never get over his turning her down. And Mary Sue still liked him.

"I didn't do anything to make him ask. You should have given him your number instead."

Mary Sue sighed. "I know. I wish I'd thought of that. He caught me by surprise."

"I'll tell him to call you. The only good thing that came out of Pete getting my number was that he talked to you. That could be a good start."

"I don't know what's so good about that." Mary Sue tried to sound nonchalant, but wasn't very successful.

"You're right. He's not good enough for you. You need someone who's wonderful and appreciates you. And it isn't Pete Milton."

"I don't think there's any chance of it being Pete Milton. He's not interested." Mary Sue forced a smile. "I'm really glad you and Mark are going out, Kaite. What are you going to wear tonight?"

It was obvious that Mary Sue had deliberately changed the subject.

"My peach-colored jumpsuit. Will that be okay?"

"It will be perfect. And call me tomorrow with all the details."

They boarded the bus for home. Kaite's heart seemed to be beating the minutes away. *Tonight, tonight,* her pulse throbbed.

She ate a quick dinner early that night and then ran upstairs to get dressed. Mom let her borrow a little of her White Shoulders perfume, and she brushed and brushed her hair so it looked soft and silky. Then she waited, sitting on the edge of her bed.

Lissa came upstairs and flopped on her bed. "What does it feel like?" Her chin was propped in her hands and she gazed at Kaite.

"What does what feel like?" Kaite resisted the urge to make a tenth trip across the hall to Mom and Dad's room to look out the window.

"To have a date with a cute boy?"

"Exciting and scary." She smiled and at the same time wished her hands didn't feel so sweaty.

Lissa rolled over, put her hands behind her head, and sighed. "I don't think anyone will ever ask me for a date."

"Mom and Dad wouldn't let you go if anyone did. You're not old enough."

"I don't mean now."

Kaite frowned at her sister. "Why won't you be asked?"

She sighed. "I never know how to talk to boys."

"You talk to them the same as other people. You talk to them just the way you do Jason."

Lissa looked up at the ceiling. "Jason and I fight. And he's not the same as boys. He's my brother. Actually, Kaite, I'm not very good at talking to anyone."

Lissa was right, Kaite thought. She hardly ever did talk to anyone—not even Mom and Dad. She was always reading. "Why don't you get a book about how to talk to people? You must know a lot of things to talk about, you read so much.''

Lissa sat up. "A book! Why didn't I think of that?'' She grabbed her current volume from the bedside table. "If I hurry and finish this, I can go to the library tomorrow. Thanks for the idea, Kaite.''

"You're welcome. I know you'll learn.'' Kaite didn't know if her sister heard what she'd said. Lissa was busy reading again.

The doorbell rang and Kaite's heart jolted. She left her room and went downstairs, trying not to rush, but finding it impossible to walk slowly.

Eric got to the door before the next ring. "Hi,'' he said. "You must be Kaite's boyfriend.''

"And you must be the booby-trap kid,'' said Mark.

Eric backed up a few steps. "Not me. Jason and Eddie.''

"You were there, Eric.'' Kaite stepped from the bottom stair tread. "Hi, Mark. Come in, please. My mom and dad are in the living room.'' She led the way, and Mark hobbled along behind on his crutch. Eric had raced ahead to announce Mark's arrival.

"Sorry about the crutch,'' Mark said, "but the doctor thought if I rested my ankle completely, it would heal faster.''

"You don't owe me an apology,'' Kaite said. It was the other way around.

When they entered the living room, she stopped so suddenly Mark almost bumped into her. Her parents sat on the couch, her mother in a beige lace dress and pearls, her father in his black suit. They were ready to go out and appeared only to be waiting for her to leave. How embarrassing! she thought. She hoped Mark didn't notice. Worse, sitting on the floor in front of her parents were the rest of the family. All eyes turned toward the two of them. She felt on display and could imagine how Mark felt.

"Um, Mom, Dad, this is Mark O'Connell."

"I've met your mom. Hi, Mrs. Grover." Mark's greeting made her feel even more stupid. He grasped her dad's extended hand and shook it. "Pleased to meet you, sir," he said.

"How's the ankle?" her dad asked.

"Still a little swollen. I'll live, though."

Kaite didn't want to discuss Mark's ankle or the accident. "And on the floor are Betsy, Eric, Eddie, Jason, and Lissa. The only one missing is PB, and that's because he's already in bed," she rattled on, anxious to get all the introductions over with.

"I don't know if I'll remember all your names, but hi," said Mark.

"Hi," the kids answered in a chorus.

Out of the corner of her eye, Kaite saw Eric poke Eddie, who poked Jason. The three of them inched their way out of the room. Maybe guilty consciences were making them uncomfortable, she thought. Well, they deserved any discomfort they were feeling, but she didn't. She was feeling jittery and her hands were starting to sweat again. She cast a pleading glance at her mother, hoping she understood.

After a few questions from her parents about school, Mark turned to her. "We'd better get going," he said.

Kaite nodded.

"Are you certain you can drive with that ankle?" Mom stood.

"Yes, ma'am. It's my left ankle and my dad's car has an automatic transmission. So I'll manage."

"Remember, Kaite, home by eleven." Dad smiled as he spoke, but for Kaite this was the ultimate humiliation. He didn't have to remind her in front of Mark! She knew what time she had to be home.

Mark winked and she couldn't help but smile. He'd probably been through that same scene at least a dozen times.

As they turned to leave, Kaite noticed Lissa peeking over the pages of her book. Her bookworm sister blushed when she saw that Kaite noticed. She glanced at Mark and couldn't blame her sister for staring. Dressed in jeans and a blue shirt under an off-white sweater, he looked terrific.

They said goodnight to Kaite's parents, then started back toward the front door. As they neared the hall closet, she heard giggles.

"He's so cute, Mary Sue!" Eddie's voice was recognizable, despite his efforts to disguise it.

"Do you think he'll kiss you?" That was Eric! His question was followed by kissing noises and Jason's laugh.

Kaite's face and neck burned with embarrassment. She couldn't even look at Mark. Yanking open the closet door, she glared down at her three brothers, who were rolling on the floor laughing. "Get out of there now!" she said in a tone of voice that was a perfect imitation of their mother when she was angry. "You're in big trouble this time!"

She heard a muffled snicker behind her.

Kaite turned to face Mark. "I . . . they . . ." What could she say?

His eyes twinkled and the corners of his mouth twitched. "Kill them later, okay? If we don't leave now, we'll miss the start of the movie."

Eric, Eddie, and Jason looked relieved.

Kaite glared at them. "I won't forget this." Finally they had the decency to look guilty.

"And let this be a lesson," Mark added. "Next time you'd better hide where there's an escape route."

"What?" Kaite sputtered as she turned to stare at him, knowing that the amazement she felt showed on her face. Whose side was he on, anyway? Hadn't he heard what they said? Maybe he was amused, but she wasn't. "Eric, Eddie, Jason, there'd better not be a next time," she said. "And if you're smart, you'll all be asleep when I get home."

"Geez, Kaite, can't you take a joke?" Eric asked as he crept from the closet.

"Yes. But you aren't funny!" She grabbed her sweater from the hanger, then hurried to the front door and yanked it open before realizing that it would take a minute for Mark to catch up.

From upstairs, she heard PB cry "Mama." The place is a zoo, she thought, feeling glad to escape.

As they went down the front walk, Mark started to laugh. "Kaite, I can almost see the smoke curling out of your ears, you're so angry."

"You'd be angry, too, if you lived in this zoo. No one deserves the six brothers and sisters I have. Those kids are . . ."

"Sure lively. I think you're lucky."

"Lucky? Lucky! Me?" Kaite knew he'd sprained his ankle, but had he also fallen on his head? she wondered.

Mark opened the door of the green compact Ford. "Try being an only child for a while, then you'll know what I mean."

"If only I could," Kaite said. "You don't know what it's like being the oldest kid in my house."

"We'll compare notes sometime." Mark closed her door and went around to the driver's side. He put his crutch in back, then slid behind the steering wheel.

Kaite turned to face him. "Better yet, I'll give you a couple of brothers and a sister, so you can experience what I go through. It's the only way anyone could understand."

Mark laughed and started the car. "Don't you think I'm experienced already?" He pointed to his ankle.

"Only a scratch," she said bravely.

"And possibly worth it," he said softly as they drove off down the street.

Kaite wished she could see his face clearly, but the shadows blocked his expression. His voice had sounded as if he meant what he said. That was too much to hope for, she decided, especially after what he'd experienced with the Grover zoo in just two encounters.

Movies were her favorite pastime. She and Mary Sue always asked to go to the movies for special occasions, like birthdays. And any time Kaite managed to get extra money, she went to the movies. These were two good ones, neither of which she'd seen.

Sitting next to Mark in the shadowy theater made her nervous. She kept glancing at him to see if he was laughing and was really embarrassed when he caught her looking. During the middle of the second movie he put his arm across the back of her chair. Kaite sat stiffly and stared at the screen. How she wished he'd put his arm around her. He was that close, but that far. Could she exaggerate when she talked to Mary Sue tomorrow and say that he'd put his arm around her in the show? If I leaned my head back . . . she thought. While all kinds of crazy thoughts and crazier wishes were racing through her brain, the movie ended and the lights came on.

"If we hurry and drive to Jack-in-the-Box, we can grab a soda and get back to your house by eleven," Mark said.

"You can't hurry with your ankle. We can skip it."

"Are you sure?"

Kaite wasn't. She didn't want the night to be over so quickly, but she'd already opened her big mouth and didn't have the nerve to take back what she'd said. She nodded.

While driving home, Mark turned on the radio. Kaite rested her head against the seat, listening to the

words of the song playing on the radio. Several lines
kept repeating in her mind:

Was our meeting really meant to be?
Could you love a girl like me?
Or are we only passing through?
Strangers tomorrow, me and you?

Was that what would happen with her and Mark? she
wondered.

They were at her house much too soon. Mark started
to open his car door.

''You don't have to walk to the house,'' she said.
''Your ankle . . .'' Kaite put her hand on the door
handle. Part of her wanted to run, but the other—the
part in charge—hesitated. She turned to face him. ''I
had a nice time,'' she said.

''Me, too. Next time, I'll be able to get around a
little better.'' He smiled.

''That's not your fault.''

''Let's not talk about my ankle.'' Mark took her
hand. He leaned toward her. His lips brushed her
cheek. ''I had fun, too, Kaite. Goodnight.''

Quickly she opened the door. ''Goodnight,'' she
said, then hurried up the walk. Her fingers shook as she
used her key to unlock the door. She glanced back.
Mark was waiting. Kaite waved, then the car pulled
away.

She touched her face where he'd kissed her—on the
cheek. She'd hoped . . . Well, what did it matter what
she'd hoped? She had a sinking feeling inside—but
wait a minute! He had said something about next
time. Maybe . . . Kaite's spirits soared once more.
Not all boys gave real kisses on a first day. Maybe next
time. Maybe . . .

Chapter Five

"I DON'T KNOW, Mary Sue. But I hope so." Kaite stretched out on the floor in her parents' room while she talked on the phone.

"He said *next time*," her friend reminded her.

"But did he mean it?"

"You have to believe he did."

"Oh, I want to." Kaite stared at the ceiling where a spider was making its way toward the wall. "But what am I going to do about the zoo? They'll ruin everything."

"You mean your brothers and sisters?"

"Of course, that's who I mean."

"Bribe them. That's what I do with my sister when I want her to do or not do something."

"Bribe them with what?"

"Money's always good."

"Of course, if I had any, which I don't. Any more brilliant suggestions?"

"Trades, threats, pleas, violence."

"Believe me, I've tried the first three. The last may be my only resort."

"With six to one? Good luck."

"I know. I'll need it."

"I have to go. My mom wants me to clean my room, and if it's not done by the time she gets home, I'm grounded every day next week. See you at the bus stop Monday. And I still think you're lucky. You may live in a zoo, but you did get to go out with Mark O'Connell."

Kaite sighed. "I know."

Saturday was cleaning day at the Grover house, too. Kaite changed her bed and lugged her dirty clothes downstairs. She and Lissa now had to do their own laundry—another new rule in their house.

Lissa was reading at the breakfast table. "Where's Mom and Dad?" Kaite asked.

"Gone shopping."

"Who else went?"

"Betsy and PB."

"Uh-oh. Where are Jason and the twins?"

"I don't know." Lissa looked up. "Kaite, did you know that lots of people are afraid to start a conversation with someone they don't know?"

"I guess."

"I'd never have believed that of Stephie Sergeant. She's the most popular girl in my class and talks to everyone."

"Lissa, there are exceptions to every rule. She's probably real confident. Read about confidence and let me know how you get some." The house was too quiet. Where were those kids?

Kaite looked out the kitchen window to the backyard. No one. She called out. No answer. "Lissa, help me find Jason and the twins."

"Check the front yard. They said something about a surprise for you."

"A surprise?" With trepidation, Kaite ran to the front door and dashed outside. "Oh, no! Stop it, you kids! Now!"

"This is going to look neat, Kaite." Jason was painting a bright yellow stripe through the middle of a huge red heart in the center of the sidewalk. Eric and Eddie were adding red arrows at each edge of the heart. Her name was written on either side—KAITE GROVER in huge red letters.

"Now all the boys will be able to find you, Kaite," Eddie said.

"Not all the boys, stupid," said Eric. "Just Mark."

"Mark already knows where I live, and he'll probably never want to come back. Which reminds me . . ." Kaite hurried toward them.

"Big mouth, Eric. Let's get out of here." Jason dropped the paintbrush into the paint can, and the twins left their paint and paint brushes on the lawn. They raced off down the street.

"Come back here and clean this up before Mom and Dad get home," Kaite shouted.

But they were too far away or they didn't want to hear.

She looked at the mess they'd made. Dad wasn't going to like this, she knew, and she suspected that some of the neighbors wouldn't be too fond of their art work, either. Well, this was one time she wasn't going to save them. Kaite turned and stomped back to the house.

"It says here that confidence is a state of mind," Lissa called as Kaite passed through the kitchen. "It means belief in oneself without conceit."

Kaite wasn't sure that helped at all. Her state of mind was in turmoil. And now there was that stupid red and yellow heart on the front walk, and Mom and Dad would probably blame her for not stopping the kids from putting it there.

The doorbell rang when she was halfway up the stairs. "I'll get it," she called, backtracking. She yanked the door open and gulped as she gazed into twinkling blue eyes. "Um, hi, Mark."

He was chuckling to himself and pointing to the walk. "Did you see that?"

"Yes and I don't think it's funny and neither will my mom and dad. Graffiti isn't approved of in the Grover family."

Mark's face grew sober. "I hadn't thought of it like that. Want me to help you scrub it off?"

Kaite sighed. "Eric, Eddie, and Jason really should be the ones to do it."

"How about if we start the job? Maybe they'll show up in time to finish. Is it water-based paint?"

"I don't know. I'll get the paint cans. They're still down on the lawn where the brats left them." She retrieved both and was relieved to see that the paint was latex, easily cleaned with soap and water. As she started back up the walk, Kaite suddenly stopped. "You don't have your crutch anymore, Mark!"

"You noticed. That's what I came over to tell you. My ankle is still a little sore, and I can't run yet, but the doctor said I could leave the crutch home as long as I wore an Ace bandage." His sock bulged over his tennis shoe.

"I'm glad," Kaite said.

His smile made his eyes sparkle. "Me, too."

"I'll go in and get a bottle of dish detergent. The hose is on the side of the house, and there's a scrub brush in the garage. I'll be right back." She ran all the way.

Mark had been right to suggest they take the heart off the walk. It wasn't an easy job and even when they'd finished scrubbing, there was still a faint outline where the cement had absorbed the color. However, he was wrong to think that Jason and the twins would show up to help. They didn't. Kaite and Mark finished just a few minutes before her parents returned from shopping.

Mom exclaimed over Mark's recovery, and Dad cautioned him to take it easy and not stand on the ankle too long.

"Come in for a Coke," Kaite insisted, hoping that all the work they'd just done hadn't made his ankle worse. Kaite's common sense seemed to have disappeared with the heart on the walk. When Mark was there, she couldn't think straight.

They sat at the kitchen table with Lissa, who kept looking at Mark, then back at her book.

"What are you reading?" he asked.

Her face turned crimson. Kaite thought she was going to get up and run. "A book on popularity," she said, "about how to talk to people."

"May I see?"

She glanced at Kaite, wide-eyed, then handed the book to Mark.

He leafed through it. "This looks good. Is it yours?"

"The library's."

"Maybe I'll take it out when you've returned it."

"But you're already popular," Kaite blurted out.

"Because I run track. But talking is a problem for me, too. When you're running, you can't talk much, but when you stop running, you have to say something."

"That's what the book says!" Lissa exclaimed. "That everyone has trouble talking sometimes."

Suddenly Kaite felt really at ease with Mark. Anyone who could admit his fears out loud was a special person. Most people claimed they had no fears, or else, that they feared something like snakes or other disgusting things that anyone could understand not liking. She rested her elbow on the table, propped her chin in her hand, and stared at Mark.

He smiled. "I have to leave. See you in school Monday, okay?"

"Okay! Sure." Kaite could hardly believe that he wanted to see her, but she was so glad he did. As she walked to the door with him, she noticed that he was limping slightly. Did Mark still want a few brothers and sisters? she wondered.

For once Kaite was eager to go to school on a Monday morning. On the bus, Mary Sue listened and sympathized as she told her about the heart. "I never did tell my parents, and if they don't happen to notice, eventually the last bits of paint will fade away. And Jason promised, no more pranks," she said.

"Do you believe him?" Mary Sue asked.

Kaite said, "I want to, but, no, I don't." She smiled.

Once again Pete Milton boarded the bus and sat across from them. "Hi, Kaite, pretty lady," he said. "What's new, Mary Sue?"

Mary Sue blushed and raised her eyebrows. "Nothing," she said.

"I hear you're going out with O'Connell, Kaite. Why not give me a chance to compete?"

"I don't think so, Pete."

"No one loves me," he complained, then swung out of his seat and sauntered to the back of the bus to talk to some other kids.

"Someone loves him," said Mary Sue. "Him."

"He is confident," said Kaite.

"He's self-assured."

"What's the difference?"

"Conceit."

"Conceit?"

"Right. And Pete's got plenty."

"Not so much that you didn't blush when he talked to you."

"Don't be silly, Kaite; I never blush."

"Instant sunburn, I suppose, that suddenly faded."

Mary Sue made a face and slid down in the seat beside Kaite. "I'm forgetting Pete Milton," she said a bit too emphatically.

Kaite nodded and wondered if she should believe her. In her opinion, Mary Sue would be better off concentrating on any other boy; but if Pete was the guy she wanted, she'd do anything to help her friend.

As soon as they were off the bus at school, Kaite started to watch for Mark. He surprised her by coming up behind her.

"Looking for someone?" he asked.

"I—um—yes. You. I wondered how your ankle was." Kaite noted the support bandage.

"Same as Saturday. Are you busy after school?"

"No." She held her breath. Was he going to ask her out again?

"I have the car today, and I could drive you home. Maybe we could study together."

"All right. I'd like that." She exhaled and smiled.

"Great! I'll meet you at your locker." He walked across the lawn and stopped to talk with a group of guys standing around the front entrance of school.

"He really likes you, Kaite," Mary Sue said as they went inside. "I'm so jealous."

"Don't be jealous. He's just being nice."

"What's wrong with that? He doesn't have to be, you know. Your brothers tripped him up. Remember?"

"Of course, I remember," Kaite said testily. "And so does he."

"You don't still have that crazy idea that he's out for revenge, do you?"

Kaite sighed. Did she? "Not really. But this all seems too perfect. Mark O'Connell, the star of the track team, wanting to date me, the star of nothing? Things like that happen in books, not in real life.''

"Don't question why. Sometimes chemistry can't be explained.''

"Tell Mr. Decker that. I flunked my last chem quiz.''

Mary Sue groaned and dropped her books in her locker. "Sometimes you are impossible, Kaite.''

Kaite ignored her friend because she was too busy wondering how she could get her brothers and sisters to make themselves scarce when Mark was visiting. She'd need a miracle and they didn't come very easily. Kaite was outnumbered and one guy could only take so much. She'd appreciate any help she got.

The bell rang and Kaite grabbed her books for the morning. If only this day could be over already, she thought. How would she ever survive a whole day of classes before seeing Mark again?

Chapter
Six

KAITE SAT PROUDLY next to Mark in his car and wondered if anyone noticed that she was with him. He'd dated lots of girls at West Valley, but none were known as Mark's girlfriend. She felt shivery inside at the thought. What if he asked her?

"Want to go for that Coke we missed Friday night?" he asked as he stopped the car at a light.

Kaite nodded.

Two more blocks and he turned the car into the parking lot of DJ's, home of the Nifty-Fifties Burger. As they got out of the car, an old Volkswagen van pulled up and three other members of the track team got out.

"Hey, I thought you guys were supposed to be at practice," Mark said.

"Without you, the team's falling apart," said one of the boys.

"What!" Kaite said, and clamped her hand over her mouth.

"Relax. He's kidding. Coach Evans canceled for

today. He's out with the flu," said the shortest of the three.

Gullible Kaite. She felt so dumb.

"When are you coming back to run, Mark?" asked the tallest boy.

"I'll be back as soon as the doctor gives the okay. Do you guys know Kaite? Kaite, this is Scott, Brian, and Chris."

Kaite felt self-conscious as they all looked at her. "Hi," she said, and knew she was blushing.

"Cute. Where and how did you meet her, Mark?" asked Chris.

She wanted to die right then. Mark looked at her and grinned. "You might say it was an accidental meeting," he said.

If I didn't love Mark O'Connell before, I do now, she thought.

DJ's decor was all Fifties. There were record album covers of the popular singers like Elvis Presley, Pat Boone, Connie Francis, and Chuck Berry in frames on the wall. Photos of the days when DJ's was a drive-in restaurant with waitresses on roller skates were arranged in a group behind the counter. There was one with a whole gang of kids sitting in and on a '55 Chevy.

"Let's sit here," said Chris.

They all squeezed into a booth, Kaite sandwiched between Mark and Brian on one side, with Chris and Scott on the other. Glancing around, Kaite saw Jackee Taylor and Monica Enright at the counter. They had turned to stare at Kaite and were whispering to each other. For a minute Kaite didn't know whether to stare back and smile or pretend she didn't see them. She decided to smile. Wait until Mary Sue hears about this! she thought. Me and four track team guys!

When the waitress came, everyone ordered Cokes except Brian who ordered milk. Chris asked the waitress why she wasn't roller-skating.

"The boss doesn't give hazard pay," she said, laughing.

"Don't you know that it's hazardous just talking to that guy?" Scott asked.

Chris poked him in the ribs, while the waitress shook her head. "I'll be right back with your drinks," she said.

At first, Kaite listened while the boys talked track and school. Gradually she relaxed and found herself laughing and joining in the conversation. Coke had never tasted so good.

"If we're going to study, we'd better get going," Mark said, glancing at his watch.

"Nice meeting you, Kaite," Chris said.

"See you around school," said Scott.

Brian smiled and waved as they left DJ's.

Kaite wished Mary Sue were there to meet him. He was really cute and seemed like Mary Sue's type, a quick sense of humor, a real tease. Mark took her hand as they crossed the parking lot. Kaite felt so happy, she wanted to sing.

"Kaite, is that you?" Mom sounded upset when she and Mark entered the house.

"Yes, Mom. Mark's with me."

Her mother came from the kitchen to the entry hall. "It's too late for me to go to the Mall now."

"The Mall?" Kaite stared at her frowning face.

"I have to buy Lissa and Jason shoes this week. You were supposed to watch the others for me."

"Oh, Mom, I'm sorry. I forgot."

"It's my fault, Mrs. Grover," Mark said. "We stopped at DJ's."

"That's nice of you to share the blame, Mark, but Kaite knows how to tell time."

"I'll come right home tomorrow, Mom."

"Tomorrow I have a PTA meeting. I'll have to put

the shoes off until Saturday. Plan to be here, Kaite.''

A feeling of resentment rose inside her. What happened to the talk they'd had? What about the new rules? What about Lissa watching while Mom took Jason? What about Jason while she took Lissa? Even though Kaite knew her thoughts were impractical, she didn't care. Orders, orders, orders. Why didn't anyone ask her? Why did she always get told? ''On Saturday, Mary Sue and I are supposed to help her mom set up the church hall for a wedding reception,'' Kaite said.

''I'm sorry, Kaite. I need you on Saturday. Mary Sue will have to get someone else to help her.''

''But, Mom . . .'' Kaite stopped and swallowed to keep from sounding like a whiny baby.

''I'll watch the kids on Saturday,'' Mark said, ''if that's all right with you, Mrs. Grover.''

Kaite glanced from him to her mother. ''Are you sure?''

''I'd love to.''

''Mom? Is it okay?''

Her mother sighed. ''I guess so. I'll try not to be long.''

''Thanks—both of you. Mom, Mark and I are going to study for a while.'' What Kaite really wanted to do was hug him. Mary Sue's mom was paying them to help on Saturday. It was one of her few chances to earn some money.

''Maybe I should leave,'' Mark said.

''No. We can study for at least an hour. I have a book report due tomorrow. Come in the living room.'' Kaite led the way. What an up and down day. One minute she was on top of the world, the next, falling from the bottom rung of the ladder. Now she was soaring again.

''Where's the zoo?'' Mark asked as they sat on the couch.

She shrugged. "If we're quiet, they might not find us."

"Kaite, I'm sorry you got in trouble."

"Mom's right. It isn't your fault, Mark. I should have remembered. And thanks for offering to help out on Saturday. If something comes up, though . . ."

"I really want to sit for your brothers and sisters."

Poor Mark, she thought. He doesn't know what he's getting into.

Kaite reached for her book, *Great Expectations*, and her notebook. Mark picked up his Algebra II book.

For a while the only sounds were the turning of pages and the scratch of pencils.

Suddenly giggles came from behind the couch. Kaite glanced at Mark and he glanced back at her, smiling. How had they missed seeing the kids sneaking in? She wasn't amused.

As Kaite turned to tell her brothers to come out of hiding, two alligator hand puppets, one green and the other purple, came up to rest on the back of the couch, almost under their noses. She started to grab one, but Mark touched her arm and shook his head.

"Hi," said the purple puppet. "My name is Kaite."

She gritted her teeth and folded her arms. She was going to regret not stopping this, she just knew it. And purple was probably a very appropriate color for her right now. She could feel the blood rushing to her face.

"Hi," said the green puppet. "I'm Mark."

"What do you want to do?" asked the purple puppet.

"Let's kiss," said the green puppet.

Kaite drew in her breath. She was right. This was too much! "All right, you two. The show is over," she said. If Mark hadn't been watching, she'd really have exploded. How much embarrassment could one sister take?

"Like this?" The purple puppet tried to bite the green puppet's nose. The two puppets proceeded to get into a fight. As usual, her brothers ignored Kaite.

"Wait," yelled the green puppet. "Kiss like this." It touched the purple puppet lightly on the mouth.

"Oh, sweetie, kiss me again." The purple puppet puckered up and turned over on its back. Then fits of giggles exploded and the puppets disappeared.

Mark smiled at Kaite. His dark hair fell softly over his forehead and his eyes sparkled with amusement. "Like this?" he asked. His arms went around her and his lips felt soft against hers.

Kaite was vaguely aware of whispers and more giggles, several *yuck's*, and the rapid departure of the puppeteers. Like that, she thought, and maybe she even whispered it. She wasn't sure because her anger had faded and she felt shaky inside. Mark pulled her even closer and kissed her once more. Back on top of the world!

"Time for me to go home," he said, moving away. He gathered his books and stood up. "But before I go, would you like to go someplace on Friday after track practice? Maybe to the Mall. We could just walk around and have dinner there, if you want."

"I'd love to, Mark."

"Great! See you at school, Kaite."

She nodded, only because she was so happy she felt like crying. Mark O'Connell really liked her!

"Mark?" Mom met them in the entry hall.

"Yes, Mrs. Grover?"

"I'm making my special pot roast. Why don't you stay for dinner?"

Dinner? With her family? Eating with the Grovers sometimes made a food fight look polite. Don't stay. Say no, Kaite focused her thoughts in Mark's direction.

"I'd like to. I do have to go home first, though. I promised to cut the front lawn."

"We eat at seven-thirty," Mom said. "Be here by then or there won't be anything left."

Kaite groaned inwardly.

"I'll come early." Mark smiled at Kaite. "See you later."

She shut the door behind him. "Mom, how could you?"

"How could I what?" Her mother was leaning toward the mirror in the hall examining her eyes. "Wrinkles," she said half to herself. "I need a bigger garden hat."

"Mom! You know what it's like at the dinner table with the kids. Can they eat early? Please?"

"No, dear. That means extra work for me."

"Can they eat in the kitchen?"

"Kaite, children learn table manners at home. That's the place to perfect them. You weren't always such a tidy eater, yourself."

"But can't they perfect their manners on someone else? Do they have to perfect them with Mark?"

"Kaite, are you ashamed of our family?"

"Well, not exactly, but . . ."

"In the next half hour, I could use help scrubbing potatoes, please." Mom went toward the kitchen. It seemed that mothers could get used to the most disgusting things, like dirty diapers and no table manners.

Rather than scrub potatoes, Kaite wanted to find a quiet spot and remember every moment with Mark from the time they left school, skipping her confrontation with her mother. After he ate dinner with them, memories might be all she had. But first she had to do something important.

She ran upstairs and looked in her room. Lissa and Betsy were sitting on the floor putting a puzzle together. "Excuse me," she said in her calmest voice. "Lissa, I'm calling a Grover kids meeting now. Do you know where Eric, Eddie, and Jason are?"

"Hiding in the closet in their room," said Betsy without looking up. "That's where they always hide." Betsy was a lot like Lissa. She didn't say much to anyone but Mom and her friend Amy, but she was certainly observant.

"Thanks. I'll be right back."

Kaite waded through a slew of outer space dolls, clothes, some schoolbooks, several trucks in pieces, and two alligator puppets—one purple and one green. Calmly but quickly she opened the closet door. "There's a meeting of Grover kids in my room," she said to the three who sat on the floor. "Right now!" Without closing the door, she went back the way she'd come. In her room she sat on the edge of her bed and waited. Jason and the twins came in right behind her.

"We were in our room when Mark was here," said Eric, immediately on the defensive.

They sat on the floor with Lissa and Betsy.

"Then why were you hiding in the closet?" Kaite asked.

"Well, he thought of it." Eric pointed to Jason.

"They didn't have to put on a puppet show." Jason defended himself and admitted guilt.

"Never mind who thought of it or who did it. These tricks have to stop!" Kaite said.

"We didn't mean to make you mad, Kaite," said Eddie.

"We thought you'd think we were funny," said Eric.

"It wasn't all my idea," said Jason.

"Was, too," Eddie muttered under his breath.

"Then why were you hiding?" Kaite asked again.

Jason shrugged. "Cause you're still mad about the other times."

Kaite slid off the bed and sat on the floor so they were eye to eye. "Listen, you guys. I know you're trying to have fun and tease me. But Mark's a nice guy and he doesn't have any brothers and sisters. He likes you, but you might make him change his mind and never want to come here again. Then I might get really mad. When he's here, I don't want to hear one more giggle or one more smart remark about kissing. And that includes tonight when he's coming for dinner. Is that clear?"

"Lissa and I didn't do anything," said Betsy.

"I know, but you can remind these three," Kaite said. "Are you going to quit?" She glared at her brothers. They all nodded.

"Promise?"

They nodded again.

"Did Mark say he wasn't coming again?" Lissa asked.

"No," said Kaite. "I told you, he's coming for dinner tonight."

"Can we leave now?" Eric asked.

"Yes. But remember your promise, especially tonight and on Saturday."

"What's Saturday?" they all asked.

"Mark is going to baby-sit."

"We're not babies," Jason said, making a face.

"He's going to stay with Eric, Eddie, Betsy, and PB. You're going with Mom for shoes."

"Where are you going?"

"To help Mary Sue's mother at church."

"What about Lissa?"

"I'm starting dance class," Lissa said.

"I thought you were getting shoes, too."

"Dance shoes."

"Mom didn't tell me that."

Lissa smiled and shrugged.

"I don't want new shoes," Jason said.

"If Mom says you're going for shoes, you're going," Kaite said.

"Now can we leave?" Eddie asked.

"Go on."

They were gone in a minute.

"Can I ask you something?" Betsy looked at Kaite.

"Sure, honey." She was the only one who wasn't giving her problems.

"Are you going to marry Mark?"

"What!" Kaite shouted so loud Betsy clapped her hands over her ears.

"If you are, I want your bed."

"Betsy, forget that idea. Forget the word *married*."

"I thought you liked Mark. Lissa, didn't you say she liked him?"

Lissa looked at Kaite and shrugged. "She's just little, Kaite," she said.

"No, I'm not!" Betsy sounded indignant.

"Finish the puzzle, you two." Kaite decided she couldn't trust any of them.

Her sisters went back to the picture on the floor.

She stretched out on her bed with her hands behind her head and closed her eyes. She thought about kissing Mark, how nice it had been. I'd better remember exactly how it felt, she thought, because after tonight and Saturday there might be no more kisses, no more Mark. Kaite sighed.

Chapter Seven

THE SMELL OF pot roast, onions, and carrots wafted throughout the house and up to Kaite's room. She stepped back from her bed and studied the two outfits left on the spread after eliminating several others. Her red shirt with her jeans? Or her turquoise shirt with her skirt? Which would be best? "Why am I worried about clothes," she asked, "when I have so much more to worry about?" Her brothers and sisters just had to cooperate, they just had to. She couldn't stand any more embarrassment.

She chose her turquoise shirt and matching skirt, then hunted in her dresser drawer for her obi belt. The belt was nowhere to be found and it was almost brand new. Chances were that it was a harness for an imaginary horse, a suspension bridge between two block towers, or a holster for a space gun for an outer space warrior. It could be under a bed, in the back of a closet, or even out in the yard attached to a tree or the handlebars of a bike. Why did her brothers and sisters think that everything that was hers was also theirs?

"No sense in getting hysterical," Kaite said to her mirror reflection. "You couldn't stand being an only child. You'd have so much time on your hands that you didn't have to spend looking for your things, you wouldn't know what to do with it all. Right? Wrong! But kids can't change what already is, especially families." Kaite took her makeup out of her drawer. She'd search for her belt tomorrow. All she wanted from her family tonight was cooperation, so they'd have a sane, calm dinner and Mark would be impressed and want to keep coming over.

She brightened her cheeks with a little blusher and smoothed eye shadow across her lids. A touch of cologne completed her dressing, but she still wasn't ready for dinner. She wasn't even hungry.

"I'm not ready. I'll never be ready." Kaite sat on her bed and wished she'd talked her mother into cancelling the dinner.

"Kaite, Mark's here." Lissa called from downstairs.

"I'll be down in a few minutes." Where had the time gone? She hadn't even heard his car or the doorbell ring. Panicky, she jumped up and stood before her dresser mirror. She stuck her tongue out at herself. Not even her hair looked good. "I know how Daniel felt before he faced those lions," she said. "But poor Mark doesn't even know that this is the den and he's probably Daniel." With a sigh, Kaite dropped her hairbrush on the dresser top and left her room.

Though she struggled to appear composed, on the inside she was a wreck as she went downstairs. Eddie and Eric were chasing each other through the living room and into the dining room, racing around the table shouting at each other. "Mark's here," yelled Eddie, as he leapt over Betsy, who was stretched out on her stomach next to the dining room table with a coloring book and crayons.

PB sat next to her, chewing on a red crayon, red wax saliva dripping down his chin. "Betsy, don't let the baby play with the crayons," Kaite called.

"I'm not. He's just taking them." Betsy took her red crayon from his tiny fist and he howled in protest.

"Betsy," Mom called, "don't tease the baby."

"He's eating my red crayon, Mommy."

"Give him something else to play with."

Betsy gave him a different crayon.

Kaite turned toward the living room, where she expected to find Mark, but he wasn't there. Her dad was reading his paper in the plush brown chair, his feet propped on the worn ottoman. "You look nice, Kaite," he said, looking over the top of the financial page.

"Thanks, Dad. Lissa said Mark is here. Where is he?"

"Try the kitchen. I think your mother roped him into helping with dinner."

"I'll look." Kaite hurried past the dining room to the kitchen. PB now held a green crayon and a purple crayon. He was drooling in Technicolor. "Betsy, take the crayons away from the baby," Kaite reminded her once more. She knew she should do it herself, but she was too eager to find Mark and rescue him, and she had no doubt that by now he probably needed rescuing.

When she entered the kitchen, she was surprised to see him sitting at the table, swirling meringue onto the tops of two lemon pies, and looking not the least bit in need of a rescue attempt.

Lissa was rinsing dishes and putting them in the dishwasher, and her mother was poking the pot roast with a long-handled fork. "Ready at last," she said, snapping shut the oven door. "Lissa, you can tell everyone to wash up."

"Hi, Kaite," Mark said. "I'm getting to be a mad meringuer." He wielded the rubber spatula; like an artist stroking oil on a canvas, Mark swirled beaten egg whites in rounded mounds with elaborate peaks.

"Are those pies ready to be browned?" Mom asked.

"I hate to give this up." Mark heaped the second pie with the remaining meringue. "I'm going to ask my mom to bake a lemon meringue pie and I'll do the *meringue*ing."

"You could bake the pie yourself," said Kaite's mom. "I'll give you my recipe. It's not hard."

"Great! I'd like to try," Mark said. "Maybe I'll become a great chef."

Kaite was speechless. Mark sat in her kitchen, talking with her mother as if he'd known her family forever. And he seemed to have forgotten all about his ankle and why it was bandaged.

"You look nice, dear." Her mother handed her a bowl of mixed vegetables. "Put some margarine on these; then put them on the table, please."

"Mom, PB is full of crayon." Lissa stood in the doorway with a squirming PB, bits of colored wax making a rainbow trail down the front of him.

"Bring him over here. Kaite, there are hot rolls in the bottom oven. Take them out, please. And, Lissa, mash the potatoes."

"What can I do, Mrs. Grover?" Mark asked.

"Take PB in the small bathroom and wash his face and hands, please." She deposited him in Mark's arms and turned to the counter where the meat platter sat.

"Come on, big boy. Let's decrayon you," Mark said. "I used to eat crayons, too, but let me tell you, they don't do a thing for you, and the flavors these days are nothing. Stick to ice cream. It's just as pretty and tastes a whole lot better."

"Ice Cweam," said PB and held his arms out toward the refrigerator.

"Pot roast," said Mark as he carried PB toward the bathroom. "That tastes good, too."

"Woast," said PB.

"Lissa, I'll finish the mashed potatoes. Be sure there are napkins and butter on the table. Kaite, after you put the rolls on the table, would you stir the gravy for me?"

"Oh, Mom."

"Turn the burner down a little if it's bubbling too much."

Mom ran a knife through the sharpener and started carving the roast.

"Mom, quit telling Mark to do things. And why can't the boys help?"

"Jason isn't home, and the twins set the table. Quit telling Mark to do what things?" Mom popped a tiny sliver of meat in her mouth. "Mmm. Not bad, if I do say so myself."

"Put meringue on the pie and wash PB and . . . It's embarrassing!"

"He's not embarrassed. I'm making him feel at home."

"I'm embarrassed."

"I don't see why. Stir the gravy, Kaite. Don't let it burn."

"He's supposed to be my friend."

"And I invited your friend to dinner and he's helping me and seems not to mind at all. You worry too much, dear. There, the roast is sliced. Let's eat."

"Did someone say eat?" Dad took the platter from Mom. "Mmm, smells delicious, looks delicious . . ."

" . . . and tastes delicious, too," Mom said, popping a sample scrap of meat into Dad's mouth.

"Only what I expected." Dad leaned down and kissed Mom.

Kaite felt like a stranger in her own kitchen. She was watching everyone do all the things they usually did, but Mark's being in the house changed it all. She was seeing what she thought he must see when he looked at her family, and she felt humiliated. Other families didn't act like hers, she was sure.

"Is PB supposed to wear a bib or something?" PB sucked noisily on his thumb as Mark carried him back into the kitchen.

"Lissa will get one for him," Mom said. "Thanks for cleaning him up, Mark." PB clung to Mark. "Kaite will show you how to put him in his high chair."

"I'll do it." Kaite put her arms out to PB, but her little brother refused to come.

"Looks as if you made a friend, Mark," Mom said, as she removed her apron.

"Is that right? Are we friends?" Mark asked PB. "Want to shake on it?"

PB took his thumb from his mouth and offered it to Mark, who pretended to taste it. "I think you should stick to crayons, pal, or pot roast. Come on, Kaite, you show me how the high chair works, and we'll get my new friend settled in for dinner."

There's still dinner to get through, Kaite thought. She wondered if she'd survive it.

PB, the twins, Betsy, Lissa, Mom, Dad, Kaite, and Mark were all at the table.

"Where's Jason?" Dad asked.

Eddie and Eric shrugged.

"I couldn't find him," Lissa said.

"He went to get some bubble gum at the store," Betsy said.

Mother started to get up, a look of concern on her face.

"I'll go look. You make some calls to his friends' houses," Dad said.

The back door slammed.

"Jason?" Mom looked relieved.

"Sorry I'm late. Mom, Dad, look what I've got. A

lady was giving them away in front of the market and . . .'' Jason appeared in the dining room door-way with an armful of reddish-brown puppy.

There was a mass evacuation from the table. Eric, Eddie, Betsy, and Lissa all jumped to see and touch the bundle of fur that squirmed in Jason's arms.

"I can keep him, can't I?" Jason asked, struggling to hold onto the rambunctious puppy.

"He can, can't he?" Lissa pleaded. "He's so soft. Come pet him, Kaite.''

"Puppy," PB said, and banged his spoon on the high chair tray.

"Jason, honey," Mom began.

"No, Jason. You may not keep him," Dad said. "Please put the dog down and wash up for dinner.''

Jason looked pleadingly at Mom. Kaite looked pleadingly at Mom, too, but not because of the puppy.

Her mother intercepted her glance. "We'll discuss this after we eat, Jason," she said. "Everyone who touched the dog, wash your hands again. Kaite, please pass the potatoes to Mark.''

Everyone was back at their places and Jason slipped onto his chair. The puppy waddled under the table, and Eric and Eddie kept leaning over to peek beneath the cloth.

Mom fixed a plate for PB and put it on his tray.

"What's that green stuff?" Betsy asked. "I don't like anything green.''

"You'll like that. It's gelatin salad," Mom said.

"It wiggles." Betsy poked the salad with her finger.

"Yeah, it's funny." Eric wiggled in his chair.

"Blup, blup, blup, blup." Eddie made appropriate sound effects as he wiggled, too, so that they bumped each other, then started to laugh.

"Like Santa Claus. A bowl full of jelly," Betsy said.

Eric got up and pretended to have a round Santa

Claus shape. "Ho, ho, ho," he said.

"Enough," said Dad. "Sit down." He passed the pot roast to Kaite, who passed it to Mark, who had become very quiet now that they were seated at the table.

The twins settled down, but every time someone passed the gelatin which started to wiggle, they giggled. Kaite tried glaring at them, but they didn't notice, or if they did, they didn't care.

"Good dinner, Mrs. Grover," Mark said as he tasted the roast.

"Thank you, Mark."

"Puppy, puppy," PB chanted, dropping some of his dinner over the side of his high chair to the waiting puppy.

"That's your dinner, PB," Mom said. "No more for the puppy. Eat your potatoes."

PB banged his spoon in the center of the mound of mashed potatoes on his plate, squishing them out to the side. He pounded again, then dropped the spoon to the puppy and picked up mashed potatoes with his fingers. He got more potatoes on his face than he did in his mouth.

"Look. PB's being gross, Mom," said Jason.

Mom wiped PB's hands and face with a napkin and handed him another spoon. "Use this," she said. "And don't play with your food, PB. Eat like a big boy."

Kaite wanted to crawl under the table with the puppy. Jason was right. PB was being gross, but so were Eric and Eddie, who started to imitate their little brother.

"Eric, Eddie, you're excused from the table," said Dad, as the phone rang.

"Kaite, will you get that?" Mom asked.

Kaite jumped up, glad to get away from the table. She tripped over the puppy, who yipped and dashed under Mark's chair as she grabbed the edge of the table for balance and upset Lissa's milk. Not bothering to look behind, she ran for the kitchen and the phone.

"It's for you, Dad," she called. Peering around the corner, while her father talked, she looked at Mark. He was eating as if nothing at all was happening, as if every day mashed potatoes flew through the air, people jumped up and down during dinner, and chaos reigned.

"I'll be right there." Her father hung up the phone. "Emergency at the hospital. Keep my dinner warm, dear." He touched Mom's shoulder as he headed for the door.

Kaite started back to the table in time to see the puppy squat near Mark's foot. "Mark," she cried, "look out. The puppy . . ." Too late. Mark looked startled as the puppy wet the toe of his tennis shoe. He pushed back his chair and held out his foot. "And my mom said they couldn't look or smell any worse. Will she be surprised."

Mom smiled, then sighed. "Jason, if you're finished eating, take the dog back where it came from. PB isn't even housebroken yet. I simply can't manage a dog, too. Kaite, get Mark a wet paper towel, please."

"Please, Mom. I'll take care of him. I'll train him."

"No, Jason."

"What if he was already housebroken? I could get a dog that already is."

"No. I want to keep this dog," Betsy said, jumping up and grabbing up the puppy in a big hug. "Please, Mommy."

"Please," said Jason.

"Please," came the chorus from the stairway—the twins, who were listening.

"He is nice," said Lissa.

"And cute," said Kaite despite herself, as she watched the floppy-eared dog kiss Betsy.

"See? He's my friend. He loves me," said Betsy.

PB stood up in his high chair and tried to reach the puppy. Mom grabbed him just in time, before he fell out.

"Kids, I like dogs, too. But I tried to explain . . ."

"The lady said I can't bring him back," Jason said, folding his arms and sliding down on the chair.

"We'll discuss it later." Mom stood up. "Everyone carries his own plate to the kitchen. Then we'll have dessert."

"I'd rather have this puppy." Betsy sounded determined.

"Mrs. Grover, what if I took the puppy home and trained him? Then would you consider keeping him?"

"Well . . ."

"Yeah, Mom. An already trained dog! I'll do all the rest of the work," Jason pleaded.

"Feeding, bathing, going to the veterinarian?" Mom asked.

"All of it, Mom. I'll even teach him to bring your garden gloves when you want them."

"My garden gloves are to be left alone. Mark, are you sure you don't want a puppy?"

"No. I think he likes this family. But I will train him for you." He glanced at Kaite. "It'll give me an excuse to come down here; you'll want reports on the puppy's progress, won't you?"

Mom smiled. "I'm sure we will, Mark, but you don't need an excuse to visit us." She glanced at Kaite, too, who blushed.

"Does that mean we can keep the puppy?" Betsy asked.

"Maybe," Mom said.

"That means yes," Betsy whispered to the puppy.

After lemon pie and coffee, everyone helped clear the table and do the dishes.

"Thank you for a delicious dinner, Mrs. Grover," Mark said.

"I'm afraid tonight was a little hectic. But the food tasted all right."

"Not all right. Fantastic!" Mark said. "Especially the lemon pie. Right. Kaite?"

"You wouldn't be fishing for a compliment, would you?" she asked.

"Not me," Mark said. "I only did the meringue."

"Ah, but you can't have lemon meringue pie without it, can you?" Kaite smiled up at him. Despite how terribly everyone in her family had acted, she guessed she'd been worrying for nothing. Mark really did seem to like all the Grovers.

She and Mark walked toward the front door. As they passed the dining room, she glanced under the table. "Mark, look." On the floor, PB and the puppy were curled up together. PB's thumb was corked tightly in his mouth and the puppy was tucked in a tight ball. Looking at them, Kaite guessed that maybe this was one of the reasons that mothers were able to put up with dirty diapers and worse. When they slept, little kids looked absolutely angelic.

"Looks as if dinner was exhausting for both of them," Mark said. "Let's talk a few minutes, then I'll take the puppy home."

Kaite glanced down at Mark's tennis shoes. "I'm sorry about how they all acted," Kaite said as she opened the front door. "You must have felt surrounded." They went outside.

Mark glanced up at a clear night sky, then drew her into the circle of his arms. "Surrounded? Only in a wonderful way. In your family, you feel surrounded by love. I can't wait to come back tomorrow and spend time with the kids."

Kaite was amazed. She looked up at him, and as his lips touched hers, she knew what he meant. She felt very surrounded by love.

Chapter Eight

FRIDAY AFTER SCHOOL, Mark met Kaite at her locker and they walked together to the track. She knew that a lot of the girls turned to look at them together, and she felt proud.

"I'm going to try the full workout," Mark said. "I'm eager to get back to running the mile. You don't mind waiting for me, I hope."

"Of course not," Kaite said. She liked watching him run. Didn't he know how good he looked in those short nylon running shorts and cutoff shirt? "I'll wait on the bench until you're through."

Mark jogged toward the gym where the dressing rooms were and Kaite continued on toward the bleachers. She sat down and waited.

When the team had gathered, Coach Evans called them into a group. "We'll start as usual with some stretches, then six laps of warm-up. O'Connell, see how you feel after that before you go on to doing wind sprints. Got that?"

"Yes, sir," said Mark. He glanced in Kaite's direction and smiled.

"What are you guys waiting for? An invitation?" shouted the coach.

Kaite watched for a few minutes, then opened her book. She had to finish *Great Expectations* this weekend. The report was due on Monday.

"Warm up," shouted the coach. "This isn't a tea party. Get the lead out."

Kaite glanced up. She felt nervous as Mark started a jog around the track. What if he hurt his ankle again? What if it hurt too much to run?

She tried to concentrate on her book, but found it impossible. Finally she closed the cover and watched the track team. Mark seemed to be running without any problem.

"Ten wind sprints now," called the coach when they'd finished the warm-up laps. "O'Connell, how are you doing?" Coach Evans had only one tone of voice, it seemed—loud.

"No problem, coach."

"All right. Go for it."

Kaite closed her eyes as they started the wind sprints, running fast. It seemed like no time at all before the coach was calling for a quarter-mile run. Could Mark do all of this at one time? she wondered. Should he?

But Mark seemed to be fine. He made it through the quarter mile and then the cool-down laps. The practice was over. Puffing slightly, Mark jogged over to her. "I'll be back in about fifteen minutes," he said. "Do you want to wait here or in the car?"

"I'm fine," she said.

"Here." He put his letterman jacket around her shoulders. "Be right back." He trailed along at the end of the team as they headed for the showers.

She wasn't cold, but Kaite pulled the jacket around her. She felt special wearing Mark's jacket; she felt like his girl.

"Ready?" He startled her out of her daydream, making her feel embarrassed. What would he say if he knew she'd been thinking about his kiss? she wondered.

"Do you still want to go to the Mall?" she asked. "After running, should you walk a lot?"

"My ankle wasn't broken, just sprained," he said. "It's just because I was using a crutch that you think it was so serious."

"If you're sure."

"It doesn't hurt. Okay?"

"Okay."

Mark put his arm around her and they walked across the field to the parking lot.

"I'm starved now," Mark said as they drove toward the Mall. "How about a snack before dinner?"

"Just something to drink for me."

"A drink is what I had in mind. Ever had Henrietta's Health Food Tropical Delight?"

Kaite giggled. "No. Is it as hard to drink as it is to say?"

"Not at all. You'll love the taste. Henrietta's will be our first stop."

Henrietta's Health Food Tropical Delight was everything Mark promised. A mixture of fresh fruit whirled in a blender, the drink was thick and delicious.

"Coach Evans discovered this. He makes us swear off junk food, but steers us toward some good-tasting stuff in place of it."

"Does he shout all the time?" Kaite asked as they strolled past the shop windows in the Mall.

"I guess. But he's nice. All the guys respect him.

That's why the team does so well. It's hard to run for someone you don't care about. Not even school spirit will make up for a lousy coach.''

They'd passed the pet store when Mark backtracked. "Let's go in and see the puppies and kittens.''

"They make me so sad. I want to buy them all,'' Kaite said, following him into the narrow shop lined with cages.

"I was surprised that you didn't have any pets,'' Mark said. "I always thought kids and pets went together.''

"They usually do, and you can tell we've been working on Mom. This time maybe we'll succeed. How is the puppy?''

"Acting just the way a puppy should. I had to look all over for my tennis shoe this morning, and he cried half the night until I let him sleep in my bed.''

"I hope your parents aren't upset because you brought him home.''

"Not at all. Mom especially is a pushover when it comes to soft, furry creatures with big, sad eyes. By the way, what should I call the puppy? It's better to train him with a name.''

"I don't know.'' Kaite thought for a minute. "How about Chaos?''

Mark laughed. "There's never a dull moment at your house, is there?''

"I'm afraid not. Chaos reigns continuously.''

"Then the puppy will feel right at home. I'll hurry to get him housebroken for you.''

They stopped to play with a beagle puppy, and Kaite tried not to fall in love with a Siamese kitten, but wasn't very successful. She cooed over the soft, furry bundle, wishing she could take him home. But that would be pushing Mom past her limit. Reluctantly she let the pet shop salesperson return the kitten to his cage.

"I have an idea. Come on." Mark grabbed her hand and pulled her from the shop.

"Where are we going?" Kaite had to run to keep up.

"You'll see."

Kaite felt like a character in a movie as she and Mark raced past shoppers and browsers in the Mall. They barely avoided several collisions.

"Mark, slow down," she said, puffing. "I'm not on the track team. Think of your ankle."

"We're here. This store closes early." He led her into The World of Toys. "On the shelf over here." Mark picked up a fuzzy stuffed animal no larger than his hand. He placed it in Kaite's hands. "A kitten for you," he said.

She held the fuzzy little kitten to her cheek. "He feels real," she said.

"I'll buy him for you."

"Oh, Mark, you don't have to do that."

"I want to." He took the kitten from her and went to the cash register.

"Thank you," she said, when he handed the bag to her. Shyly she slipped her arm around his waist and hugged. He hugged her back.

"Shall we look for a place to eat?" he asked.

"Are you hungry already?"

"Not already. Still. I'm just a growing boy. Ask my mom." Mark laughed.

"All right. Let's eat," Kaite said. "I don't want Coach Evans any more upset with me than he has been. What would he say if he heard I'd starved his star runner?"

"Whatever he says, he'll say it loudly," Mark said. He hugged her again.

They chose the Pucci's From Italy restaurant. Kaite ordered lasagna and Mark chose ravioli.

"Is this dinner on Coach Evans's list?" Kaite asked

as they left the salad bar.

"We aren't expected to starve," Mark said. "In fact, just before a big meet . . . the coach wants us to eat lots of food like spaghetti and bread. It's called carbohydrate loading. Then we run it off."

"You'll work this off tomorrow, if you're still going to stay with my brothers and sisters. Or do you have to do something else?" Had he forgotten? Would she have to tell Mary Sue she couldn't help at the church?

"No, I didn't forget. I run early in the morning. I'm looking forward to staying with the kids."

Kaite shook her head. Mark was a glutton for punishment, she decided.

When they'd finished eating, they walked through the Mall for a while, looking in shop windows, talking about school and their families. Kaite felt comfortable with Mark. She wanted to know everything about him.

Mark glanced at his watch. "Time for me to take you home. I have to start a term paper tonight, though I wish I didn't. I'd much rather keep walking and talking with you."

"Me, too," Kaite said.

Mark put his arm around her, and she put hers around him as they walked to the car. The sky held just a faint hint of orange where the sun had set. When they were in the car, Mark didn't start the motor right away.

"Kaite, I like you a lot," he said. "More than any other girl I know."

"I like you, too, Mark." Kaite felt smiley, yet she felt teary, too. She guessed that was because she was so happy.

He leaned toward her and kissed her, their lips lingering in a gentle touch that made her heart pound. He kissed her forehead, then with a sigh started the car.

Kaite leaned her head back on the seat and closed her eyes. If this was a dream, she didn't want to wake up. Mark was so wonderful. He made her feel special and maybe he'd ask her to be his girlfriend. She wouldn't say no.

In her lap she held the toy kitten Mark had bought for her. She'd had no problem naming him. She called him Maybe.

Chapter
Nine

IT SEEMED STRANGE to leave the house on Saturday and see Mark's car parked in front. He'd helped the twins set up the croquet set in the backyard, and when Kaite left, everyone, except PB, who was watching from his play pen, was playing croquet. She hoped Mark could keep peace between the twins and would have the patience to explain to Betsy how to play the game.

She walked the five blocks to Mary Sue's house, then they rode with her mother and her little sister Tricia to St. Andrew's Church.

While they set up tables and chairs, Mary Sue's mother took Tricia to visit Mr. Deems, the minister. "I'll be arranging the altar flowers," she said, "while you girls work in the hall. You know where the chairs and tables are stored, don't you?"

"We know what to do, Mom. Don't worry," Mary Sue said. They hurried into the church hall. Mary Sue turned on the lights and they set to work.

Kaite related her Mall date with Mark. "You have to

see the kitten. It looks absolutely real, Mary Sue. It's
so cute!''

"So is Mark. You really like him a lot," her friend
said.

"More than a lot." They dragged a long table across
the room.

"Has he kissed you yet?"

Kaite nodded. She could still remember how nice his
kisses had been.

"What did it feel like?"

"Nice."

"I know, but can't you be a little more specific?"

"No." Kaite's face felt warm, and she hurried to the
closet to get some chairs.

"Kaite, I'd tell you."

"What's Kaite supposed to tell?"

Kaite jumped as she turned to see Pete lounging in
the doorway.

"What do you want?" Mary Sue asked.

"What a warm welcome," Pete said sarcastically as
he sauntered into the church hall and straddled one of
the chairs.

"Why don't you give us a hand instead of just sitting
there?" Kaite asked.

"If I do, will you let me drive you home?"

"Pete, what are you doing here?" Mary Sue asked,
not giving Kaite a chance to answer him.

"Trying to get Kaite to let me take her for a ride.
Also, I brought my mother over to practice the organ.
There's going to be a wedding tonight."

"No kidding," Mary Sue muttered under her
breath. "And what are you practicing?"

"Nothing. What is this anyway, Mary Sue, twenty
questions? Do I win a prize if I answer them all right?"

"Yeah. You win me." Mary Sue slammed a chair
under the table. She sure reacted violently whenever

Pete was around, Kaite thought.

"How about it, Kaite?" Pete ignored what Mary Sue said, causing her to slam a few more chairs. "Finish here and I'll drive you home."

"I don't know, Pete." Kaite glanced at her friend. Maybe she could help Mary Sue.

"Let him," Mary Sue said. "If he drives you home, you'll get there in time to help the baby-sitter, if you know what I mean. Mom will probably be here all day."

"Pete could drop you off at home, too," Kaite said.

"I doubt he'd want to." The look in Mary Sue's eyes told Kaite that was exactly what she'd like.

"Pete, will you drive both of us?" Kaite asked.

"Sure. Why not? If you're sure Mary Sue won't bite."

Mary Sue slammed another chair.

"She won't. Grab another table," said Kaite.

With the three of them working, by noon the hall was set up, the floors swept, and the tables decorated. Kaite tried to imagine how the bride would see their work. The neat white tablecloths hung evenly. The wedding bell decorations needed only the flower sprays added on each side to be complete. Mary Sue's mother would add them later, so they wouldn't wilt. The longest table was set up for the wedding gifts. And the kitchen was clean and ready for the caterer. Kaite hoped the bride would be pleased. If it were her wedding, she would be.

They asked Mary Sue's mother if they could go with Pete. Since she and Mrs. Milton were good friends, she agreed.

"Be sure to remind Peter that he has to be back at two to drive me home," his mother said, when she was told that he was leaving.

"I'll tell him," Mary Sue answered.

The Miltons' Jeep was bright red. Without thinking, Kaite climbed in the back. Pete looked at her and frowned. So did Mary Sue.

"Your house comes before mine, Mary Sue," she said. "Get in."

Pete turned on the radio. He raised the volume so they couldn't talk without shouting. After several attempts, Kaite gave up.

When they reached her house, Mary Sue got out quickly. "Thanks. And don't forget to pick up your mother." She slammed the door.

"Call me later," Kaite shouted, but her friend didn't look back. What's wrong with her? Kaite wondered.

"Come up front, Kaite. I don't want to play chauffeur." Pete patted the back of the passenger seat.

Kaite eased between the bucket seats and plopped into the seat beside him. Pete backed the Jeep out of the drive. As she looked toward Mary Sue's house, Kaite saw her friend peeking from the bedroom window. Kaite waved, but Mary Sue didn't wave back.

"What are you frowning about?" Pete asked.

"Um, nothing." Kaite turned around. She'd call Mary Sue as soon as she got home.

"Are you busy tonight?" Pete downshifted as they came to a light.

"I think so." Kaite wished he'd quit asking. She couldn't wait to get home. She hoped Mark was still there.

"Mmm," Pete said, and accelerated so quickly she had to grab onto the seat.

"Slow down."

"Sorry. Didn't mean to scare you." He grinned.

"I'm not scared. Why don't you ask Mary Sue if she's busy?"

Pete looked at her and shook his head. "Because I want *you* to go out with me. What time should I pick you up?"

"No time. I said no." Kaite stared out the window. Thank goodness Mary Sue and I live close together, she thought. Pete seemed to show off in every way he could, including driving. Her father would have plenty to say if he saw her riding with him, even if Mary Sue's mother had said it was okay.

"Where do you live?" he asked.

"Berkley Drive. The second house on the left," Kaite said when he neared her street.

He turned quickly, making her grab for the door. "Pete, quit that."

"Nothing will happen. Stay calm. I'm a good driver."

Kaite was glad when he stopped in front of her house.

"Last chance. Are you busy tonight?" he asked as she opened the door.

"Pete . . ."

"Kaite, Kaite, Kaite." As she stepped from the car, Betsy, wearing a baseball cap that almost covered her eyes, grabbed her in a big hug. "I can play croquet. Mark helped me and I won! I beat everybody!" She let go of Kaite's legs and jumped up and down clapping her hands excitedly. "Come and see how I can hit the ball." She tugged at Kaite.

"Just a minute." Kaite tilted the cap back from her eyes then took her hand. "Thanks for the ride, Pete."

"One more chance," he said.

"Hey, Kaite, come on. We're going to put Lissa's giant puzzle together. You can help." Eric ran down the front walk, followed a minute later by Eddie and Jason. "Mark and Lissa are turning over all the pieces. Hurry!"

"Mark is still here?" Pete was so distracting that she hadn't looked to see if his car was still there. Kaite was glad, but surprised. Jason and Lissa's being there meant Mom was home.

"He's been waiting for you," said Jason.

"Looks as if the whole neighborhood is waiting at your house today," Pete said sarcastically. "Including O'Connell. Come around to my side of the car. I want to ask you something, Kaite."

"Pete, they're not the neighborhood, they're my brothers and sisters. And whatever you want to know, just ask me here."

"It's about your friend, Mary Sue," he said. "Come over here." He crooked a finger at her.

Kaite was curious. Maybe this was another chance to help Mary Sue. "Stay here, Betsy," she said. Leaving her little sister on the curb, Kaite ran around the Jeep. Maybe he was going to take her suggestion and ask Mary Sue out. When she stopped beside Pete, he opened the door and leaned toward her as if was going to whisper something in her ear, but instead he kissed her. "More and better next time," he said, laughing and quickly closing the car door.

Kaite put her hand to her mouth. "You . . . I . . . What about Mary Sue?" She wanted to throttle Pete Milton. A dozen names she didn't dare say out loud strangled her.

"Tell her next time she'll have to get her own ride home." Pete gunned the motor. "I'll call you."

"Don't bother," she shouted. "Don't . . ."

He waved and accelerated so quickly the twins jumped back and Betsy ran toward the porch.

"How come you let him kiss you?" asked Jason, who was left standing by the curb.

"I didn't." Kaite stepped out of the street and watched the Jeep race down the street. What did Mary Sue see in Pete Milton? she wondered. "Let's see about that puzzle." Boiling inside at Pete's unbelievable egotistical nerve, she started up the walk. She was almost at the steps when she glanced toward the porch.

An unsmiling Mark stood there holding PB. "You're still here," Kaite said and smiled.

"And you didn't think I would be," he said sarcastically.

PB started to cry and wriggle.

"I'll take him." Kaite put out her arms and PB came to her. "I'm glad you didn't leave, Mark."

"Really? Why? So I could see Milton's wonderful red Jeep?"

"Oh, he just gave Mary Sue and me a ride home from church. His mother was there practicing the organ and—"

"I saw what he gave you." Mark spoke quietly.

Kaite felt her face burn. Darn! Why did she have to blush now?

"He kissed her," said Eddie.

"Eddie! It wasn't that way. He—"

"Well, he did."

Eric, Jason, and Betsy stood behind Mark nodding and looking accusingly at her.

"You don't understand," she said, feeling her face burn even more.

"You don't have to explain to me, Kaite. We hardly know each other." Mark's eyes looked cold as he stepped past her. "I should get home. My folks might have something they want me to do."

"But the puzzle," said Jason.

"Another time," Mark said. "And tell your mom I can't stay for dinner after all. Sorry."

"But we want you to," said Betsy, running after him. Her baseball cap flopped from her head onto the grass, but she didn't stop to pick it up.

He ruffled her hair. "Not this time. Better get your cap."

"Mark, wait." Kaite started off the porch after him.

"Sorry, can't." He jumped in the car, and as he

backed from the drive, there was a loud clattering sound. With a surprised look he pulled forward, but the sound came again. He turned off the motor and jumped out. Getting down on his hands and knees he peered under the car. Moments later he reached under and pulled out a rope to which was tied a can, a sand pail, and several old tennis shoes. He ran around to the back of the car, untied the rope, and tossed it onto the lawn.

"Who did that?" Kaite asked as she watched helplessly. Every movement he made indicated anger. But when she looked back toward the porch, she was alone, except for PB who had snuggled against her and was working on his thumb.

"Mark, I'm sorry about the rope. I'm sorry about Pete. Please let me . . ." Mark slammed the car door, then drove away without a backward glance or a toot of the horn. " . . . explain," Kaite finished softly.

Filled with feelings that made her feet seem to weigh a thousand pounds, Kaite trudged back to the house. Inside, she put PB in his playpen, said hello to her parents, and went to the phone. She dialed Mary Sue's number.

"Mary Sue, I have to talk to you," she said.

"I thought you were my friend. That was real cute, Kaite. You get in the back and let Pete take me home first so you can have him all to yourself. What about Mark? You don't need two boyfriends."

"Mary Sue, you know me better than that. It wasn't like that at all."

"I thought I knew you, but I'm not so sure. You should have seen yourself at church. *Come and help, Pete.*" She imitated Kaite. "And I suppose you're going to tell me he didn't ask you out, either."

"You know how he bugs me. You've been there. I told him no, Mary Sue, and . . ." Kaite knew from the muffled sound on the line she shouldn't have admitted the truth. "I didn't even think about who went home first. Your house was closest and—''

"He could have gone to the farthest house first— your house. He had to go back to the church to get his mother. My house is closest to church. You didn't think of that, did you? Today was my chance, and you took it away.''

"No, I didn't.'' Kaite felt her temper rise, too. She'd had all the false accusations piled on her she could take for one day.

"You did. He even had time to come in if he'd taken you home first, Kaite. But, no. You arranged it so I'd be dropped off first.''

"Mary Sue! What's the matter with you? You can't possibly believe that. I can't stand Pete Milton. If you must know, I think he's a creep.''

"Thanks for telling me I have such good taste,'' Mary Sue said coolly. "And here I was apologizing for giving him your phone number. I knew that was a mistake, but I didn't know why until now. I watched you flirt at church. I'll never believe you when you say you aren't interested in a boy ever again. I guess you like *creeps*, too.''

"You have it all wrong. You're overreacting.''

"Overreacting? Don't accuse me of overreacting. I know who my friends are and you're not one of them, Kaite Grover.'' Mary Sue hung up.

Bewildered and feeling the threat of tears, Kaite raced up the stairs. She threw herself on her bed. What had happened? She'd started out to do a favor for her friend and ended up with both Mark and Mary Sue angry.

"It's not my fault,'' she sobbed into her pillow. "It's not.'' She tried to think of one of the little prayers that ordinarily came so easily to her when she needed help, but the words wouldn't come to her. Everyone seemed to have abandoned her. Only Maybe, with his green glass eyes, seemed the same.

Chapter Ten

"KAITE? MOMMY SAYS to come downstairs. Daddy fixed chicken on the barbecue outside."

Kaite opened her eyes to see Betsy standing in the bedroom doorway. Her littlest sister stared solemnly at her. "I didn't mean to make Mark mad." Her lower lip poked out and she wiped a fist across her eyes.

Swinging her legs over the side of the bed, Kaite went over to Betsy and put her arm around her. "You didn't make him mad, honey. I did." Or rather Pete did, she thought.

"Uh-uh." Betsy shook her head, sending her blond pigtails twirling. "I told Eddie to put the rope on the back of his car. Mark didn't like that."

"You?" Kaite shook her head. "No, he didn't like that. Betsy, don't you remember our meeting? All of you promised to leave Mark alone."

"We promised not to say anything to him. I didn't say anything, Kaite." Betsy smiled, her tears subsiding as quickly as a spring shower. She could look so angelic sometimes.

Kaite sighed and straightened up. She sat on the edge of her bed again. "Where did you get the idea to tie a rope full of junk on the back of his car, anyway?"

"From TV. I thought if I put the cans on his car, he might want to get married to us and play croquet all the time. But I'll tell him I didn't mean to."

"Never mind." Kaite dragged herself to the dresser where she peered into the mirror. Her face was blotchy and her eyes were puffy. She pulled a brush through her hair. "Tell Mom I'll be right down. And forget about Mark. He probably won't be around again after today." It hurt to say those words out loud, and Kaite's tears threatened to spill over again. She wished—well, she wished a lot of things. But she especially wished she'd never seen or heard or talked to Pete Milton.

"Kaite?" Betsy hadn't left.

"What?"

"Will Mark keep our puppy?"

"Oh, honey, I don't think so. I'm sure he'll bring the puppy back as soon as he's trained. Don't worry about that."

"You're sure? You said he wouldn't come around anymore."

"But he'll bring the puppy. He just won't stay." It was the only thing Kaite felt sure about at the moment. Mark liked Betsy and the other kids, even if he didn't like her any longer. That thought hurt to the very center of her. Kaite bit her lip to keep from crying again, because she knew she'd have to face the family at dinner.

Paper tablecloths flapped on the picnic tables that were set up in the backyard. Mom bustled back and forth from the kitchen with plates, cups, milk, and a large platter of corn on the cob ready to go on the fire. Lissa carried the tray with the salt and pepper, napkins, and silverware. The twins were playing with a Frisbee back by the big oak tree. Jason was holding a platter for

Dad, who was turning the chicken. The smell of bar-
becued chicken made Kaite's stomach growl. How can
I feel so bad and still be hungry? she wondered. She
hurried to help her sister arrange the plates and silver
on the tables.

During dinner, she ate in a daze, answering questions, talking with her parents, but inside she carried a
heaviness that wouldn't go away. Without Mark and
especially without Mary Sue, her world felt out of
kilter.

Sunday arrived sunny and warm. The Grovers filled
a whole pew in St. Andrew's Church. Kaite was con-
scious that only a few rows back Mary Sue sat with her
family, too. The seat felt hard under her, and she
inhaled the cool, candle-and-starch scent of church and
thought about her friend. Several times Kaite turned
around to look and once caught Mary Sue looking over
the top of her hymnal directly at her. They both looked
away quickly. Kaite hoped Mr. Deems would preach
about forgiveness, but instead he was talking about
honoring your parents, which seemed to make all the
parents in church very happy.

As soon as the service was over, Kaite got her
mother's attention by tapping her arm. "I'm going to
try to catch Mary Sue," she said. "I'll meet you by the
car."

"Don't be too long, dear," her mother said.

"I won't be." Kaite squeezed from the pew and
hurried down the aisle. She tried to ease past the slow
walkers and catch up with Mary Sue, whose parents
were now shaking hands with Mr. Deems by the
church door. She made herself inconspicuous behind
two heavyset women and rushed past the minister. It
wasn't that she didn't like Mr. Deems. The round-
faced man with his thin hair and pink cheeks was very
nice. But Kaite knew if she stopped to talk with him,

he'd keep her there until her parents arrived. Meeting the congregation was one of Mr. Deems's favorite Sunday pastimes.

Slightly ahead of Kaite, Mary Sue preceded her parents down the three church steps and started across the parking lot. Kaite caught up with her. "Hi," she said. "We have to talk."

Mrs. Cariatti smiled. "We'll wait in the car, but don't be long, you two." She slipped her hand under Mr. Cariatti's arm and they continued on.

Mary Sue looked surprised. "There's nothing to say. Did you come to church hoping to see Pete? He isn't here. He hardly ever comes."

"I always come on Sunday, and I never want to see Pete Milton again. I wish you'd believe me. I only wanted to get you two together. I never even thought about having him take us home in a different order. I always think of myself as living farther than you from church. Honest, Mary Sue, I don't like Pete. And if it will make you feel any better, Mark got angry when he saw that Pete brought me home and he left and I haven't heard from him, either." Saying it out loud made Kaite feel even worse.

"What am I supposed to do about that? Going home with him was your idea. You're the one who said yes." Mary Sue's voice and attitude were still cool.

Kaite stopped walking. "Then you really meant it when you said I wasn't your friend?"

Mary Sue looked down. She moved her foot over the pavement making a small arc in front of her. "I don't know," she said softly. "Maybe you don't like Pete, as you say, but I do, Kaite. I've wanted to go out with him for a long time. But he always asks someone else and now you and—and I don't know if I can stand it. I guess I just blew up."

"I said no. And I'll keep on saying no, even if Mark

stays mad at me. I'll even try to help you get Pete, if that's what you really want.''

"I guess you really are my friend." Mary Sue turned toward the car. "I'm sorry I yelled at you."

"I'm sorry, too. I should have told Pete we didn't want a ride at all."

"But we did! I did! And I liked sitting next to him in front. The ride just wasn't long enough." Mary Sue's face turned scarlet.

Kaite remembered the mean things Pete had said about her friend. "Just don't get your hopes too high. Pete . . . well, Pete is just Pete. We can try to get him to ask you out, but try not to be too disappointed if he doesn't. Okay?"

Mary Sue nodded. "If he just got to know me, he'd like me. Don't you think?"

"Everyone who gets to know you likes you," Kaite agreed. But Pete isn't everyone, she thought. She wasn't sure Pete had room inside to like anyone but himself. Still, if her friend still wanted to go out with him, she'd do whatever she could to make that happen.

Mary Sue's parents were already in the car when they reached it.

"Kaite, I didn't have an opportunity to pay you for helping at church yesterday. I understand from Mr. Deems that the wedding and reception were beautiful." Mary Sue's mother fumbled in the bottom of her purse.

"He always says that," said Mary Sue's father.

Her mother smiled. "Here, dear." She handed Kaite a five-dollar bill. "Thank you."

"Thank you," Kaite said. "Will I see you in the morning, Mary Sue?"

"Why don't you come over later this afternoon?" Mary Sue said. "I have the new Thompson Twins tape."

"I'd love to." Kaite smiled, then ran to her car, arriving the same time as her family. It felt good to have her friend back again. She only hoped that she was doing the right thing, promising to help Mary Sue get a date with Pete Milton. She thought he was the wrong boy for her friend, and yet if that was what her friend wanted . . . Friends helped each other, no matter what. Didn't they?

In her purse Kaite had the new eye shadow her mother had bought to replace the one her brothers had ruined, her coral nail polish, and some new gray eyeliner. She hurried up the front walk to the Cariatti house.

Dennis was washing his car in the drive. "Hi, Kaite-did. What did you do?" he teased.

"None of your business, Dennis," she teased back. He was already in college and really cute. When she was in junior high, she'd had a crush on him, but he'd never looked at her twice. Now he was just like a brother to her.

"Go on inside. My mom and dad went to look at new cars. Mary Sue is probably in her room. And whatever you did, don't do it again."

Kaite grinned and opened the door. The Cariatti house always looked so neat. She didn't think her house had ever looked as much like a model home as Mary Sue's did. In a way it looked as if no one lived there. Mrs. Cariatti even had fresh flower arrangements in the entry, living room, and dining room. Kaite felt as if she should tiptoe and whisper.

"Mary Sue, where are you?" she called, softly at first, then a little louder.

"Upstairs. Come on up."

Kaite didn't touch the polished wood banister as she climbed to the second floor. Mary Sue's room was to the left. She had her own room and so did her little sister. Kaite couldn't imagine having so much privacy. It must be wonderful, she thought.

Mary Sue's room was decorated in a rainbow of pastels, very soft and feminine. She was stretched out on the pale pink carpet reading the new issue of *Miss Teen*. Her cat, Princess, was curled on the chair in the corner, occasionally swishing her tail at her mouse dreams. Kaite thought about her cat, Maybe. He was the only kind she'd ever have at her house.

"I'm trying to pick a new way to wear my hair," Mary Sue said. "How do you like this?" She turned to a page where the model had short, curly hair. "Or this?" She turned to a longer frizzy look.

"That's a drastic change. Are you sure you want such a complete new look?"

"The old me isn't getting anywhere."

"You're talking about Pete."

Mary Sue nodded.

Kaite dropped onto the floor beside her. "Are you sure about Pete, Mary Sue? I mean, he's kind of conceited and . . ." She stopped as she saw the look in her friend's eyes. "I'm your friend, and I just don't want you to get hurt." Kaite had already been hurt. She thought about Mark and wondered how she was going to talk to him.

Mary Sue nodded and turned the page in the magazine. Kaite realized that she didn't want to talk about Pete Milton.

"I got some new eye shadow and gray eyeliner. Want to experiment?"

"You brought them?" Mary Sue sat up. Makeup was a safe topic. Kaite opened her purse. She'd hoped to talk to Mary Sue about Mark, but she guessed she couldn't, not without talking about Pete, too.

"Uh-huh. And some nail polish, too."

"Let me see."

Kaite held out the eye shadow case and the bottle of nail polish.

"Oh, yummy colors. Mind if I try this blue?"

"That's why I brought it. Let's go for exotic."

They sat together on the bench in front of Mary Sue's small dressing table with the lighted mirror and experimented with the eye shadow. Mary Sue had some green eye shadow and some purple. They made stripes and dots on their eyelids and giggled at some of the results and were surprised at others.

As the afternoon passed, Kaite felt that she had a friend again.

"I have to leave," Kaite said. She blew on her nail polish trying to make it dry faster.

"Are you going to wear this eye shadow to school Monday?" Mary Sue asked, peering into the mirror.

"Probably. Why don't you wear the purple?"

"Okay. Maybe Pete will notice."

Kaite smiled. "Maybe he will." Would Mark notice if she wore the blue shadow? Would he even look at her?

Kaite was glad that Pete wasn't on the bus Monday morning. Beside her she could sense Mary Sue watching when they got to his stop and felt her disappointment when he didn't board the bus. "You'll see him at school," she said. "You know he usually doesn't ride."

"Except lately . . ." Mary Sue sighed.

Kaite stared out the window and wondered if she could patch things up with Mark as easily as she had with her friend. Talking with him about Pete wouldn't be as easy as talking with Mary Sue. She didn't know about the stolen kiss. And Kaite had known Mark such a short time, only long enough to know that she liked him a lot.

The hustle and bustle in the school halls was the same as on any Monday morning. Kids raced down the halls. Groups gathered to talk and laugh. Books were dropped with a clatter into lockers. The metallic opening and closing of doors echoed over the buzz of conversations.

When she reached her locker, Kaite was dismayed to see Pete waiting for her. She ignored him as she turned her locker combination and yanked the door open.

"Busy this weekend?" he asked.

"Yes. I'm busy this weekend and every weekend for the rest of my life." She tried to catch Mary Sue's eye. Maybe Pete would ask her instead. But Mary Sue had her head in her locker and was searching for something.

"You're cute when you're angry." Pete leaned an elbow on the locker next to hers.

"Pete, you've been watching too many movies. Whatever role you're playing, drop it. I'm not impressed. I don't want to go out with you now or ever. So quit asking me." Kaite rummaged in the bottom of her locker for her books. She glanced down the hall and saw that now Mary Sue was watching and listening. She motioned for her friend to come down. Mary Sue seemed to take forever to close her locker and walk the few feet down the hall. She clutched her books in front of her.

"What am I going to do?" Pete asked. "You won't even give me a chance, Kaite."

"What are you going to do? I'll tell you what. Meet a nice girl, someone who will appreciate you. Pete Milton, this is my friend Mary Sue Carriati. Mary Sue, Pete Milton."

"I already know Mary Sue," said Pete, not even saying hello to her.

"Get to know her better. Ask her out. I'm not going anywhere with you."

"Was O'Connell upset Saturday?" He grinned, and Kaite had a sinking feeling in the very pit of her stomach.

"That's none of your business," she snarled.

"He saw us kissing, huh?" Pete winked. "Too bad. Can't he take the competition?"

Kaite heard Mary Sue's intake of breath. "No, he didn't see *us* kissing," she said. "He saw you taking advantage of me and misinterpreted. And you're no competition for Mark O'Connell. You never were, Pete."

"She really loves me," said Pete, looking right at Mary Sue. "What more can I say?" He kept grinning as if this were the biggest joke in the world. Kaite wanted to shove his grin right down his throat.

She looked at him unbelievingly. He thought he was some kind of leading man, the way he was talking and acting.

"What more can anyone say?" Mary Sue said in an even voice. "I forgot something in my locker." She turned away.

"You are despicable, Pete Milton!" Kaite slammed her locker door and raced after her friend.

"I'll call you later," Pete shouted, loud enough for half the school to hear.

Kaite didn't answer. She was too angry. She caught up with Mary Sue in the girls' bathroom. "Will you let me explain, please?" she asked.

Mary Sue slammed her books down on the edge of a sink. "I thought you already had on Sunday. But you forgot to tell me everything, didn't you? No wonder Mark is mad."

"Why do you listen to what Pete says, but not to what I say?" Kaite asked. "He's on some kind of fantasy trip. He acts as if he thinks he's Tom Cruise, Rob Lowe, and Simon Le Bon all rolled into one. I'm supposed to fall at his feet. I'd laugh if he didn't make me so sick. Mary Sue, do you hear me?''

The other girls in front of the mirror had stopped combing their hair and putting on makeup, and were watching and listening to them.

''I heard you on Sunday.'' Mary Sue yanked a brush through her dark hair, then dropped the brush into her purse. ''And I believed you—then.'' She grabbed her books and pushed past Kaite to the door.

''I didn't want to hurt you,'' Kaite said.

''Ha!'' Mary Sue opened the door so hard it banged into the wall. She stomped out of the bathroom. ''You should have thought of that on Saturday.''

''Were you talking about Pete Milton?'' asked Josie Cameron. She was one of the prettiest, most popular girls in school and captain of the cheerleading squad. Everyone liked her.

''Don't mention his name to me,'' Kaite snarled.

''Pete Milton,'' Josie said, nodding. ''Couldn't be anyone else. He's bad news.''

''At least he pretends to be,'' Kaite said.

''No. He is. Believe me. It isn't all an act,'' said Josie.

''I wish someone would tell Mary Sue that. She won't listen to me.'' Kaite took a tissue from her purse and blew her nose. Once again she felt close to tears.

''I can tell her plenty. I went out with him once. It was like dating a whole football team, but I was the only one playing defense,'' said Josie.

''I hope she'll listen,'' said Kaite, but she had her doubts. Mary Sue seemed to be blind and deaf where Pete was concerned. And she'd promised to help her get a date with him. If she went back on her word, there would be no hope for their friendship. Yet, after talking with Josie, should she help Mary Sue date Pete? Kaite felt trapped. What was she going to do? If only there was some way to make Mary Sue see what Pete was really like.

Chapter
Eleven

HER BOOKBAG WEIGHTED her shoulder, making Kaite's body feel as heavy as her heart. All during the school day, Mary Sue had managed to avoid her. If she hurried, she might be able to catch her on the bus. There, she'd have to listen.

She pushed open the school door and ran right into someone coming in. "Sorry. I . . ." Her words faded as her eyes met familiar blue ones. "Mark."

"I'm late for track practice," he said and held the door for her. "I left my shirt in my locker."

"Can't we talk even for a minute?"

"Not now." He stood waiting for her to come out the door so he could go in.

With a sigh, she stepped past him. The sun was bright and traffic raced past on the Boulevard, but Kaite felt cold and she had little energy.

"Kaite?"

She turned around slowly, hoping he didn't notice the tears that glistened in her eyes.

"We're running a meet tomorrow. Will you come to watch?"

"I . . . Yes. I'll come."

"Maybe we can talk after. I have to go." He stepped inside the school and let the door close behind him.

Feeling much lighter than she had moments before, Kaite hurried down the walk. The bus was pulling away just as she got there and, despite her shouts, didn't stop. She sighed. Now there was hope that Mark would listen to her, but as for Mary Sue, she didn't know.

At home, Lissa was waiting for her in the bedroom. "Did you see Mark today?" she asked.

Kaite nodded. She dropped her bookbag on the floor and sat on the edge of her own bed. "I'm going to the track meet tomorrow. He said we'd talk after. I'm going to try to explain about what happened Saturday."

"What did happen?"

Briefly Kaite told her sister about Pete.

"What a rat! Didn't you want to punch him?"

"Most definitely, and I'm sorry I didn't think fast enough to do just that."

"He'd better never come around here," said Lissa.

"That's for sure," said a voice from the doorway. Kaite turned to see Jason. He stood with his hands on his hips and his feet apart, a miniature Superman.

"Believe me, I'm not inviting him," said Kaite, feeling a rush of love for her protective siblings. "Where's Mom?"

"Out back weeding the vegetable garden."

"Aren't you supposed to be helping, Jason?" Lissa asked.

"Aren't you supposed to be setting the table for dinner?" he countered, sounding like his usual self again.

"I'm going to talk to Mom. You two settle what

you're supposed to be doing.'' Kaite hurried downstairs and out into the yard.

"Hi, honey. How was your day at school?" Mom, with a large straw hat pulled down over her forehead, was hoeing between the rows of vegetable seedlings.

PB sat on the ground nearby, pulling grass by the fistful and putting it in a pail.

"Fine, Mom. Hey, Pooh, we won't have to cut the lawn when you're through.''

"My pail,'' said PB, holding up the red plastic bucket.

"I know.'' Kaite sat on the grass beside him. "Mom, tomorrow after school there's a track meet and . . .'' She stopped as she saw the look on her mother's face. "Where are you and Dad going?"

"I have a doctor's appointment. But I suppose Lissa and Jason . . .''

"Please, Mom. Mark is going to run. I want to watch him. It's really, *really* important.''

"That important? I think I'm having a hard time letting you grow up, Kaite," she said. "All right. I'll take Pooh with me, and Lissa and Jason can be in charge of the twins and Betsy for the short time I'm gone. Next time I'll make an earlier appointment.''

"Next time?" Suddenly Kaite realized what her mother had said. "Why are you seeing the doctor? Mom, you're not—''

"No, I'm not going to have another baby,'' Kaite's mother laughed. "I'm seeing the doctor for my pap smear. Nothing serious, dear.'' She smiled.

Kaite breathed a sigh of relief. "Mom, when you were my age, did a boy ever keep asking you out that you didn't want to go out with?"

"More than once. But it's a good idea to date more than one boy. You're too young to get serious.''

Kaite was about to object, but had second thoughts. There was no one she could get serious with right at the moment, not even Mark. She knew she blushed at the thought and became suddenly busy helping PB pull grass.

"This is a boy who isn't so wonderful, Mom. And worse, it's a boy Mary Sue likes and wants to go out with."

"Why would Mary Sue want to date a boy who's not so wonderful?" Her mother scuffled the hoe back and forth between rows.

"Because she thinks he *is* wonderful. It's so complicated, Mom."

"It does sound that way. Don't let PB eat grass, please."

Kaite took the grass from her baby brother's mouth and put the pail back in front of him. He got up and went to dig in the garden.

"Time to take him inside," her mother said, removing her garden gloves. "Bath time, Pooh Bear." She lifted him off several flattened vegetable plants.

"I'll put the hoe and your gloves away, Mom."

"Thank you, dear. And all you can do about this boy is keep saying no. But I wouldn't encourage Mary Sue to go out with him if he's not very nice."

"That's what I thought." Kaite sighed. Yet, she'd promised. She'd never broken a promise to Mary Sue before. Maybe this had to be a first time. She just didn't know. She continued to mull over her problem as she walked to the garage.

The stands were crowded for the meet the next day. Kids shouted back and forth and waved tiny school banners. The Pride Club sold popcorn and soda to raise funds for the school.

Kaite's heart beat just a little faster than usual, whether from the excitement of the crowd and the competition of the meet or from watching Mark run, she wouldn't admit. He wore maroon running shorts and the maroon and gold school colors on his shirt.

His best event was the mile. His sprained ankle hadn't seemed to affect his time too much. Mark was one of the fastest in the high-school competition. West Valley High was way ahead, and Coach Evans was shouting encouragement, as usual.

Kaite stood in front of the bottom row of bleacher seats and sipped from her large cup of Coke. She was warm and slightly hoarse from cheering.

"Hello, Kaite, feisty lady." The greeting and a hand on her shoulder startled her.

She looked behind and was eye to eye with Pete. Quickly, she turned back, but not before she caught a glimpse of Mary Sue sitting several rows up and slightly to the right in the bleachers. She put up a hand to wave, just as Pete stepped down to squeeze in beside her. "Go away," she said. "I don't even want to talk to you." Kaite turned at a slight angle so she wouldn't have to look at Pete. She tried to concentrate on the final event of the meet.

"Aw, come on, Kaite. What are you so steamed about? A friendly little kiss?"

"We are not friends, Pete. Leave me alone."

"I can't. You're fun, a challenge." He put his arm around her waist.

"I'm not fun. And get your hands off me." Kaite leaned close to Pete to speak so she wouldn't make a scene. Her Coke sloshed on her hand.

"I'll take you to a movie tonight and afterward we can get to know each other. I'm fun and friendly, too." He tried to pull her even closer.

Pete and his dumb charm boy act! Kaite couldn't stand it. She'd show him that when she said to leave her alone, she meant it. So that it looked completely accidental, she leaned toward him, going with the pressure from his hand, and let her Coke spill down the front of his cotton pants.

"Hey! Watch it!" Pete jumped, jostling the girls on the other side of him. "Look what you did!"

"Quit pushing," said one of the girls.

"There's no room here," said another.

"Butt out," said Pete, brushing at the stain on his pants.

"Oh, I'm *so* sorry. You must have distracted me so much, I didn't know what I was doing." Kaite spoke in exaggeratedly apologetic tones.

"You dumb . . ." Pete swallowed the rest of his sentence. How quickly his charm faded.

"What's going on?" Mark, with a towel around his neck, stopped a few feet from Kaite. He glanced at Pete. "Sorry I couldn't get over to say hello before."

Had he seen what happened? she wondered. If Pete spoiled everything when she and Mark were just starting to talk again . . .

"You were terrific," she said, wishing she didn't sound so falsely cheerful. There were a million other things she wanted to say, all of them churning inside her. Especially, she wanted to say, Please talk to me. Please understand. Instead she smiled.

"Thanks. I guess you've been enjoying the meet okay, Kaite," Mark said, and there was no understanding in his voice or in his eyes.

"She's been having a wonderful time," Pete said, his voice like syrup.

Kaite glared at him. He was getting even for the Coke bath. "Mark, you were—"

"Well, I have to get back. Coach Evans doesn't like us to get too far away," Mark interrupted. His voice sounded impersonal.

"Mark," Kaite called, but he didn't turn around, "where shall I meet you after the meet?"

Mark kept on going.

"Pete, I wish I'd drowned you in Coke." Kaite

didn't wait for him to answer or for the meet to end. She felt empty inside, as she ran from the bleachers and across the school parking lot. All she wanted was to get home and find a quiet place to cry, if there was such a place in the Grover house.

The phone was ringing when Kaite reached home. She wondered where everyone was. The house seemed deserted. She grabbed the receiver off the kitchen wall as the jangling continued. "Hello."

"Kaite, this is Mary Sue."

"Oh, Mary Sue. I've been trying to talk to you ever since—"

"I think it's just terrible what you did to Pete Milton at the game."

"What!"

"He told me how he tried to keep you from getting bumped when everyone was cheering, and how when you saw Mark you spilled your Coke down the front of him, so it would look like you weren't there with him. If you're going to go out with Pete, Kaite, at least you could be honest with Mark."

"I'm honest with everyone," Kaite protested. "If you're looking for honesty, you shouldn't listen to Pete Milton. Let me tell you what really happened."

"Never mind. He already told me."

"Mary Sue, you're absolutely blind! You actually believe him instead of me?" A dial tone hummed in Kaite's ear. What she said as she slammed down the receiver would have made Mr. Deems blush and her parents angry. She didn't care.

Why doesn't anyone listen when I tell the truth? she wondered. She walked up the stairs as if they were the steepest mountain in the world.

The phone rang again when she reached the second floor landing. Kaite crossed her fingers in hopes that it might be Mark calling. "Hello?" she said, trying to sound calm.

"Is this Kaite?" She didn't recognize the voice, but it was a girl.

"Yes."

"This is Josie."

"Oh, hi." What did she want? Kaite wondered.

"I tried to catch you at the meet, but guess I missed you. I'm having a party next weekend. Can you come?"

"Well, I—"

"No couples. Lots of kids. I'm inviting Mark O'Connell, if that helps you decide."

"I'll come."

"I thought you would. Dress casually. And bring any tapes you like. I'll give you my address at school."

"What about food?"

"Sure. Bring food, if you want."

"All right. Thanks for asking me."

"Oh, do you have Mary Sue's phone number?"

Kaite gave her the number, then hung up. She wondered how many kids would be at Josie's party. What did it matter? she thought. Mark would be there and maybe she could talk to him at last. Mary Sue, too, if she went.

Kaite picked up Maybe, her kitten. "Everything was so wonderful when Mark bought you for me," she said. "Now everything is so awful. Will Mark ever care about me again? And what am I going to do about Pete? He won't leave me alone."

The back screen door banged. Moments later, she heard the twins quarreling. Betsy and Amy were singing along with a record player in Betsy's room. She guessed Mom was outside in her garden. PB was probably there, too, pulling more grass to fill his pail. And who knew where Lissa and Jason were.

Despite the sounds and activity that surrounded her, Kaite felt very alone. Throwing herself across her bed, she poured out her troubles to the small stuffed animal.

Chapter Twelve

KAITE DIDN'T WANT to wait until the party to make up with either Mary Sue or Mark. But Mark seemed to do an exceptional job of avoiding her in school, and phone calls did no good, either.

After school, she went to Mary Sue's house. Mrs. Cariatti answered the door. "Hello, Kaite," she said.

"Is Mary Sue home?"

"She's taking a bath, dear. Would you like to come in and wait for her?"

"Yes, thank you." Kaite stepped past her. The house smelled of furniture polish. "May I wait in her room?"

"Yes. Of course."

Kaite went upstairs. She sat on the edge of the bench near the dressing table and remembered their recent makeup session. When she looked up, Mary Sue was standing in the doorway, a towel wrapped around her. "Get out of my room. Who said you could come in here?"

"Mary Sue, I want to talk to you."

"There's nothing you can say. Mom, I'm out of shampoo," Mary Sue called. "Go home, Kaite." She turned and went back to the bathroom, slamming the door behind her.

Kaite knocked on the door. "What Pete said isn't true."

Mary Sue turned on the water and didn't answer.

With a sigh, Kaite went back down the stairs. "Mrs. Cariatti, I have to get home. Ask Mary Sue to call me, please?"

"Of course, dear."

Kaite walked slowly. She felt empty inside.

Not one to give up easily, Kaite continued to call her friend, but without luck. Several times Kaite went to track practice in hopes of talking with Mark. When she got there the Friday before the party, the team was doing stretches. Brian sat on the lower bleachers, watching.

"Hi." Kaite sat beside him and scanned the rows of boys, trying to find Mark.

"He's not here."

Kaite looked down at her hands clenched in her lap and sighed. "Oh. Brian, why aren't you exercising?" she asked, afraid to ask where Mark was but dying to know.

He didn't smile as he looked at her. "I pulled a back muscle. Have to take it easy for a few days," he said. For a minute he seemed to study her, his frown deepening. "What are you doing here, Kaite? I thought Pete Milton was your boyfriend now, and you wouldn't catch him getting sweaty. It's none of my business, of course, but why you'd choose him over Mark I'll never know. Mark really liked you, you know."

"That's not fair, Brian."

"Tell me about fair," he said. "It seems as if you

keep flaunting Pete in Mark's face, and he doesn't understand why.''

"But I haven't! You've heard Mark's side of the story. How about listening to mine? That's fair."

"All right. Tell me what's so wonderful about Pete Milton.''

"Nothing!" Quickly she told Brian what had happened both times Mark had witnessed her and Pete together.

"So why haven't you told him?"

"Because he won't listen to me. In fact, he keeps avoiding me. I came here hoping to have a chance to talk to him.''

"The doctor wanted to check his ankle to see how it's holding up after running.''

Kaite folded her arms. That ankle! She still felt embarrassed about the whole episode in front of her house. "Would you tell him I was here?" she asked. "That I have to talk to him?''

"Sure. I'll see him tomorrow night at Josie's party. Aren't you going?"

"Yes. And Mark's definitely going?"

"He said he was. And then you can tell him yourself. That's going to be some blast. She must have invited half the school. It'll be a good chance for you two to get back together." Brian sounded more relaxed, friendlier.

"I'm not so sure," Kaite said as she stood up to leave.

"See you then," Brian said. "And I'm sorry I believed that you and Pete . . ." He ran his hands through his hair as if embarrassed.

"I'm glad someone finally believes me," said Kaite. "See you at the party.'' She felt only slightly less discouraged as she walked toward the bus stop.

At home, Mom was working in the garden again. PB was in his playpen, banging the top of his bucket with a wooden spoon. Lissa had gone to the library. Betsy was at Amy's house. "Where are the twins and Jason?" Kaite asked. Any time those three were missing, she felt nervous now.

"They're playing somewhere inside, I think," Mom said. "How was your day, honey? You're late getting home." She pushed a strand of hair back from her face, leaving a dirt streak across her forehead.

"My day was okay. I stopped to watch track practice."

Her mother straightened up from the row of onion sets she was putting in. "Any special reason? Planning to join the team? Working out for the next Olympics?"

"You know why, Mom." Kaite sat down on the grass and plucked a fluffy white clover.

"I didn't mean to upset you with my teasing," said Mom.

"You didn't. Mark wasn't there. The doctor wanted to check his ankle."

"His ankle. Is that what's bothering you? I'm sure Mark isn't holding a grudge."

"I still feel embarrassed about his ankle. But it's more than that." Kaite shredded the clover into a dozen pieces.

"Do you want to talk, honey? You've been moping around here for days."

Kaite sighed. "Remember that boy, Pete, I told you about?"

"The one who wasn't so nice?"

"Yes. He was putting his arm around me at the track meet, and Mark saw him and thought I liked him. Mary Sue is still mad at me, too. I'm on everyone's bad list, Mom. And I didn't do anything to get there."

"Did you do anything to get off?" Her mother smoothed the dark earth over the tiny onion bulbs.

"Everything I could think of. I tried to explain to both Mark and Mary Sue. I even called Mary Sue and went to her house. She won't talk to me, Mom. And I thought we were friends. Now I wonder if I was the only one who felt that way.''

Her mother brushed the dirt from her gloves. "It's more difficult for some people to say they're sorry than others," she said. "If Mary Sue's your friend, you'll have to be patient. Eventually, she'll want to talk to you, too.''

"I hope you're right, Mom. Maybe at the party tomorrow night . . .''

Her mother put her arm around Kaite. "I hope I'm right, too. Good friends are hard to find. And speaking of the party, what do you have to take?''

"My Billy Joel tape and any kind of food.''

"I have some leftover asparagus," her mother said.

"Mom, you know what I mean." Kaite laughed for the first time in days. It was a good feeling.

"If your brothers haven't found them, there are some fudge brownies in the cupboard. Put a big RE-SERVED sign on them and take those.''

"Thanks, Mom. I'll check right now." Kaite gave her mom a hug and ran toward the house.

As she opened the door, she gagged. "What is that awful smell?" she yelled. "Jason? Eric? Eddie? Where are you? What are you doing?''

"Geez, it's Kaite. Dump it now." Jason's voice came from the laundry room.

Kaite hurried across the kitchen. She pushed the window above the sink open wider. The smell was even stronger. She put her hand over her mouth and nose. "What are you kids doing?''

She heard the glub-glub of something being poured from a container, then the sound of water as the faucet in the laundry room tub was turned on.

"Jason, answer me now.''

"Did you call me?" Jason stepped from the laundry room trying to look innocent. Behind him came Eddie

and Eric. Both of them coughed, and Eddie kept his
hand over his nose.

"What's that smell?"

"Smell? What smell?"

"You know what smell."

"Maybe it's PB?" said Eddie.

"PB is outside with Mom." Kaite pushed past them
and opened the laundry room windows. "What did you
kids mix together?"

"Some old perfume and a few other things from the
garage," Eric muttered.

"What old perfume?"

Jason shrugged. "Some stuff from your dresser."

"Some stuff? I don't have any *old* perfume!"

"Smelled old to me," said Eric.

"I thought you were told to stay out of my room and
leave my makeup and things alone."

"We were doing it for you, Kaite," Eddie said.

"Doing what for me?"

Jason nudged the twins with his elbows.

"Jason, what does he mean?" Kaite moved toward
her brothers. They backed up. "Jason? Eddie? Eric?"

"We were just making a magic potion so Mark
would come back."

"Magic potion?" Kaite felt some of her anger slip
away. "I'm afraid it will take more than magic," she
said.

"This one was a love potion," Eddie said.

"Shh!" Both Eric and Jason hissed at him.

"Oh, no. I told you guys . . . Did you dump all of
it? You didn't put it anywhere on anything, did you?"

Jason shook his head and looked down at the toes of
his shoes, already looking worn. "It smelled too bad."

Kaite sighed. Thank goodness, she thought.

"We like Mark. Can't you get him to come over to
see us, even?" Eddie asked.

Kaite tried to hug all three of her brothers at once,

but they squirmed from her grasp.

"Geez, do you suppose smelling that stuff makes you feel lovey?" Eddie asked.

"If it does, you three are immune," Kaite told them. "And I can't make Mark do anything. But no more tricks, even if you mean well. Okay?"

Jason shrugged, while the twins both muttered an okay.

Early Saturday morning, Kaite put her hair up in rollers. She ironed her blue cotton jumpsuit and borrowed her mother's blue bracelet. She was nervous about going to the party, but eager to get there.

She wished Mary Sue had called. Usually they shared the excitement of going to a party or a dance. Tonight, she'd probably have been riding with her friend, too. Now she had to get a ride from her mother. How embarrassing!

Even though Kaite had her driver's license, her parents wouldn't let her drive at night yet. "Maybe this summer," her father said, each time she asked. Kaite tried to be patient, but she sometimes wished she didn't have to wait for and plead for everything she wanted to do. Being the oldest seemed like being part of an experiment. Mary Sue got everything from her parents so easily. "Because Dennis paved the way for me," she said. "He had to fight for it all." It didn't seem fair.

"Mom, I'm ready," she called, picking up her purse and heading for the stairs.

"Can we ride with you?" asked all the kids.

"Sure," said their mother before Kaite could voice her objection. Just what she needed—to arrive at the party in the zoo wagon. But the kids were already out the door.

Josie lived in the foothills of the Santa Monica

Mountains. The evening was clear and cool. From Josie's house, the lights of the San Fernando Valley spread out like a sparkling carpet below.

Mrs. Grover stopped near the drive of a two-story wood and stucco house. "What time should I come back?" she asked.

"I'll call you, Mom. Maybe Mary Sue will give me a ride home." Kaite noticed her friend's car across the street. She also spotted the red Jeep. Why had Josie invited Pete? Now she'd have to spend the evening avoiding him. She was almost tempted to go back home while her mother was still there.

"Don't be too late."

"I won't." Kaite knew she sounded upset.

"Hey, look," said Betsy. "There's Mark. Mark! Mark! Hi!" She hung out the window and waved.

"Mark! Hi! Hi!" The others took up the call.

Mark waved and jogged toward them. Kaite clasped the package of brownies and looked down at her feet. All these days of wanting to talk to him and now he was so close and she couldn't say even a hello.

"Hi, Mrs. Grover. Hi, kids. Hi, Kaite." Mark smiled.

"You look all healed," said Mom.

"The doctor gave me my walking—or should I say running—papers. I'm good as new."

"When are you coming over?" Eddie asked.

"How's our puppy?" Betsy leaned halfway out the window.

Mark pretended to punch Eddie in the nose, making him grin. Betsy tried to grab his hand. "The puppy is fine. He's getting smarter every day. I'll bring him over one day soon."

"There's no rush," Mom said.

"He's really very smart, Mrs. Grover. You'll see." He turned to Kaite. "Shall we see who else is here?"

She realized she was staring at him. "I . . ."

"Oh, I forgot. Maybe you were supposed to meet someone in front?" Was it a question or was he being sarcastic? she wondered, looking away. He was still angry, she realized. He'd been hiding it in front of her family.

"No. No one. I'll walk in with you, if that's okay." She turned back toward the car. "I'll call you if I need a ride, Mom."

"Remember, not too late."

"Why can't Mark drive Kaite home?" Jason asked.

"Never mind, Jason." As usual, Kaite wanted to strangle her brother.

"He could," added Eddie. "He knows where we live. Don't you, Mark?"

"That's enough," said Mrs. Grover. "You can call me, Kaite."

"But, Mom . . ." began Eric.

Kaite was grateful when her mother eased the car away from the curb.

"Bye, Mark. Bye." The kids waved as the car moved away. Kaite could hear her mother scolding and telling them to sit down, put on seat belts, and pull their arms back inside the car.

"Sorry," she muttered as she turned toward the house.

"Your mother won't have to come," Mark said.

Kaite's heart seemed to jump. Did he mean . . . She looked up into cool blue eyes.

"I'm sure Pete will be glad to drive you," he added, dropping back slightly.

"I'm sure he wouldn't be." Kaite stopped before they reached the gate and turned to face him. "And if you'd listen to me for two minutes instead of running away every time you see me, you'd know that's the truth." From the other side of the redwood fence, rock music-beat. Shouts and laughter rang in the evening air. Kaite clutched the package of brownies and stared up at Mark.

"I'm not blind, Kaite." Mark reached past her and pushed open the gate.

As he swung the gate inward, the first thing Kaite saw was Pete Milton dancing with Mary Sue. Pete saw her, too. He glanced at Mark and grinned. "I'll save you a dance, Kaite," he called.

Kaite glanced up at Mark. He wasn't smiling back. And when she looked back at Mary Sue, her friend was glaring daggers at her.

"I'll find Josie," Kaite said half to herself. She wished she'd stayed home. What was the use of explaining to Mark and Mary Sue? They didn't want to hear the truth. They'd both judged her and found her guilty.

Chapter Thirteen

THE CAMERONS' YARD was the perfect setting for a romantic party. The slope at the back of the lot bloomed with tangles of sweet-smelling jasmine. Large tubs of red geraniums made shadowy mounds at the corners of the patios. Paper lanterns were strung between the posts that supported the latticed patio cover which stretched the length of the house. A kidney-shaped pool, edged with brick, created bluish, wavery shadows from the light at the deep end. The spa at the shallow end bubbled and steamed like a witch's caldron.

A few couples sat on the benches around the edge of the garden. Some had their arms around each other and one or two were kissing. Others were gathered in groups talking while a lot danced on the pool deck and the brick patios. Even though the party wasn't couples only, many of the kids paired off as if it were.

Kaite hurried past them, feeling alone and left out. Mark seemed to melt into the shadows. She scanned the crowd looking for Josie and spotted her on the far side of the kidney-shaped swimming pool, part of a talking, laughing crowd. Kaite hurried toward her.

"Brownies! Yummy!" said Josie when Kaite handed her the package. "These won't last long."

"That's for sure. Pass them over here." Brian reached out to take the package from Josie.

"I'll help eat them," said Chris. "How are you, Kaite?"

"Fine," she said, forcing cheerfulness she didn't feel into her reply.

"Mark is coming tonight," said Brian.

Kaite felt the burn of tears in her throat. She nodded. "Josie, may I go comb my hair?" she asked.

"Sure. I have to get these brownies onto the food table and give everyone an equal chance," she said. "Let's go."

"Not fair," called Chris.

"Hey, guys, there's Mark over by the tape player. He told me he was going to bring his Lionel Richie tapes." Scott lifted the package of brownies out of Josie's hands as he passed. "I can sniff out chocolate brownies a mile away," he said. "Thanks."

"I give up!" Josie laughed and let the package go. She pushed her long dark hair over her shoulders. After calling greetings to several new arrivals coming through the gate, she turned to Kaite. "Come inside."

The mellow romantic sounds of Lionel Richie echoed in the night air as Kaite followed Josie through the sliding doorway. They entered a paneled family room carpeted with dark brown shag carpet. Colorful posters and photographs decorated the walls. "The bathroom is across the room to the left," Josie said, then turned to go back outside.

Kaite entered the small bathroom. The wallpaper was printed with turn-of-the-century newspaper ads. She took a minute to read the praises of oil for well-groomed hair and mustache and the offers of cannons, whalebone corsets, and washboards for sale.

Looking in the mirror, she fluffed her hair. The curls were already falling out. What difference did it make? She'd wanted to look nice for Mark and he hadn't even noticed. Misery looked back as she tugged a brush through her hair. "Why can't I make him understand?" she whispered. Inside she was past ache and heading for numb. What had seemed to be developing into the perfect romance was never going to be, she thought. Not only would Mark never be her boyfriend, but she'd lost her best friend, too. And it was all because of Pete Milton's inflated ego, his stupid romantic hero act, his determination to push himself at her. The only girls he didn't seem to bother were those who fell all over him or those who really liked him, like Mary Sue.

Kaite stopped brushing. Was that the answer? Even if she didn't have a chance to mend her relationships with Mark and Mary Sue, she'd do anything to get Pete to leave her alone. Suddenly she realized how she might do it. What did it matter if everyone thought she had fallen for him? That's what she wanted him to think, too. Then, if he followed his usual pattern, he'd stop pursuing her and maybe he'd even go after Mary Sue. They had been dancing when she'd come into the party. What was there to lose? She'd lost what had mattered weeks ago.

Kaite finished brushing her hair, put some lipstick on, and forced herself to smile. "Pete Milton, you wanted me," she said. "You've got me."

Leaving her purse on the piano in the family room, she returned to the yard. When she stepped through the doorway, she glanced toward the sound of laughter. Josie, Mark, Chris, Scott, and Brian were standing together. Josie put her hand on Mark's arm, and he bent to listen to her. Then he put his arm around her shoulders and hugged her lightly. Kaite forced herself to smile, despite the ache inside.

"Ready for that dance?" Pete came up to her and grabbed her hand. He pulled her toward the shadows near the tape player.

"Sure. I haven't danced since I got here." Kaite went along without protest.

Someone had substituted a Cyndi Lauper tape for Lionel Richie. *Time After Time* started as Pete pulled Kaite into his arms. He held her so close she could hardly breathe.

"You finally decided to be nice," he whispered in her ear. His hand moved down her back and came to rest at the base of her spine.

If she could only pretend he was Mark . . . but that seemed impossible. As he tried to pull her even closer, she had second and third thoughts about leading him to believe that she could tolerate him at all. He gave her the creeps. "I've always been nice." She tried to create some space between their bodies by leaning back slightly.

"I know." She guessed from the way he drew out his words that he was trying to sound sexy. To her, he sounded stupid. He stopped dancing as the song ended. "Let's sit down." He put his arm around her shoulders, letting his hand fall on the front of her jumpsuit.

"Forget it, Pete," she said, wiggling out from under his arm. "I thought we were going to dance some more."

"In a while. Don't be so uptight. I want to show you how nice *I* am." He turned her to face him and kissed her.

"Pete!" Kaite pushed him away, but he grabbed her hand.

"Quit teasing," he said. "You know you like me.

And O'Connell isn't exactly falling over himself to get to you."

"I want to dance." Kaite felt as if she was going to cry. This was a stupid idea. She wished she'd never started it. She tried to walk away and he followed her.

"All right. One more dance. Then let's get out of here. This party is one big bore. But first, another kiss."

Kaite knew how the victim of an octopus felt, as she saw Pete's hands reaching for her. She backed away from him, but he was insistent. She put her hands up to keep him at a distance, but he grinned and kept coming. "Leave me alone, Pete," she said. "I said I wanted to dance, nothing else."

"You're a tease, Kaite," he said.

"Pete, I mean it." She struggled to keep her voice low. She didn't want to attract attention.

He lunged for her and Kaite reacted. As she jumped out of his way, Pete lost his balance and fell face first into the swimming pool.

He gurgled curses at her as he surfaced.

"Just shut up, Pete! I hope you drown." Shouts and laughter rang in Kaite's ears as she raced toward the house and took refuge in the bathroom.

What kind of story would Pete tell when he got out of the water? She didn't even want to imagine. It was sure to be something terrible. Something everyone would believe. Kaite sat on the toilet and rested her head in her hands. Tears she'd been holding back too long trickled through her hands and dotted the legs of her jumpsuit.

"Kaite? Kaite, are you in there?"

Quickly Kaite brushed her hands across her eyes. She jumped up and turned on the water. "What do you want?" she called as she dabbed at her red, swollen eyes.

"It's Mary Sue. I have to talk to you."

Kaite blotted her face and dried her hands, then opened the door. Mary Sue stepped inside and closed the door behind her. For a minute they stared at each other.

"It's true, isn't it?" she asked.

"If it's something Pete said, probably not." Kaite couldn't help but sound defensive.

Mary Sue looked away. "I guess I deserved that answer. What I meant was, it's true that it was Pete coming on to you all this time, not anything you were doing."

"Yes, it's true. Why didn't you believe me, Mary Sue?"

"I wanted to, sort of." She leaned against the counter. "But, Kaite, I thought I really liked him. He's so cute and he wouldn't even smile at me. And then he kept talking to you and asking you out and—"

"And I said no. Do you remember that?" Kaite asked. "He's awful, Mary Sue."

"He's so good-looking."

"True. But he doesn't have any friends."

Mary Sue frowned and looked down at her shoes.

"Both of us know how important friends are. And you don't just get friends. You have to work at being a friend first. And I don't think Pete knows how," Kaite said.

"I guess you're right. Poor Pete." The girls hugged again. "You know, I was jealous," Mary Sue said.

"Was?"

"Tonight when the guys dragged him out of the pool, he started saying how you were begging him to kiss you and that he was trying to get away and . . ."

"Lies!" said Kaite.

Mary Sue touched Kaite's arm. "I know. That wasn't you at all. And you should have seen Mark. He was really angry. Pete left when he saw that he wasn't getting any sympathy. Kaite, no one believed him. And Josie said if anyone was begging, it was definitely him.''

"She said that in front of everyone?''

Mary Sue nodded. "I'm sorry, Kaite.''

Once more they looked at each other. Then they were both smiling, though Kaite's smile was still teary.

"Sorry enough to give me a ride home?'' Kaite asked. "I hate to have to call my mom.''

"Of course, I'll give you a ride. Unless Mark offers.''

Kaite sighed. "I wouldn't plan on that.''

"It's never too late. Put some lipstick on. Then let's go back outside. The party isn't over.''

"Is there any food left?'' Kaite asked. "Suddenly, I'm starving.''

"It's the athletic workout you've just been through.'' Mary Sue giggled.

Kaite joined in, though she still felt somewhat embarrassed at the thought of facing everyone. What if they asked for the details?

Josie was the first to come up to her at the food table. "I'm sorry I invited Pete Milton,'' she said, "but I'm glad you dumped him in the pool. He deserved that and more, I'm sure.''

Kaite nodded. She looked around the yard. Mark wasn't anywhere she could see.

"Mark left right after Pete did,'' Josie said.

"Oh.'' Kaite turned back to the table so she wouldn't see how disappointed she was.

"Maybe he'll come back,'' said Mary Sue, scooping the dip from the bottom of the bowl with a potato chip.

Kaite didn't answer. Maybes never seemed to work out for her—except one. She thought about the cat Mark had given her.

Scott asked Mary Sue to dance. Kaite went to sit on a

bench and watch. Gradually kids were leaving the party. Mary Sue's giggle echoed over the sound of the music. Kaite smiled. She'd have chosen Brian for her friend, but she realized that even though they were best friends, she and Mary Sue had different taste. But that was okay, she decided. She knew what could happen if they both liked the same boy.

Mrs. Cameron came outside and said that it was time to turn off the music. "We don't want to upset the neighbors," she said.

Kaite and Mary Sue and a few others helped carry the little bit of leftover food inside, and Scott and Brian carried the record player, tape deck, and speakers in.

"Mark didn't come back," Mary Sue said. "I'm sorry."

Kaite sighed. "Me, too."

As she climbed into the front seat of her friend's car, she couldn't help but wish that it was Mark who was taking her home. She rested her head on the back of the seat and closed her eyes. She felt as if she were on a seesaw, one minute up and the next down. She wondered if it would ever be possible to balance again.

"He might call you," Mary Sue said.

Kaite didn't answer. She was remembering that she'd seen Mark put his arm around Josie and hug her. If he was going to call anyone, it was probably Josie Cameron.

Chapter Fourteen

"KAITE, LOOK!" As Mary Sue slowed her car near the house she pointed to the car parked in front—a green Ford.

"What's Mark doing here?" Kaite blurted out.

"Can't you guess?" Mary Sue smiled as she pulled her car to a stop across the street from Kaite's house.

"He probably wants to ask about Pete. Mary Sue, you tell him what happened. I don't want to talk about it anymore. I just want to forget all about Pete Milton."

Mary Sue sighed.

"Oh, I'm sorry. I forgot that you like Pete. I didn't mean . . ."

"Yes, you did. And the word is *liked*," Mary Sue said. "I guess I found out what he was really like tonight, too. And Josie gave me a pretty good description of what a date with him is like. I guess I was only looking at how cute he is, not at what he's really like—the inside person. Actually he was doing me a favor by ignoring me. I just didn't know it.''

"I wish he'd done me the same favor," Kaite said. "But now you can concentrate on Scott."

"Who?"

"Don't sound as if you don't know who Scott is. I'm sure he'll remind you so you can't forget."

"Mark saw my car. Here he comes, Kaite. I'd better leave. My mom will be pacing the floor if I'm not home right on time."

"Thanks for the ride—and everything."

"Thank you for wanting to be my friend again."

"Kaite, can we talk for a minute?" Mark opened the car door for her. In the light from the street lamp his face looked very serious.

"All right. Goodnight, Mary Sue."

"Goodnight. And call me tomorrow. Okay?"

"Sure."

Mark took Kaite's arm and they walked toward his car. From one of the trees a mockingbird sang a nighttime medley. A gentle breeze made the leaves rustle and blew Kaite's hair around her face. She brushed it from her eyes. "Would you sit with me for a couple of minutes?" he asked, as they neared his car.

Kaite glanced toward the house. She'd called from the party to let her mother know she had a ride home. A small light burned in the entry hall and the porch light twinkled a welcome. "I guess I can." She felt fluttery inside as he held the car door open for her. What would he say?

For a minute he sat behind the steering wheel and stared straight ahead. Kaite was aware of the beat of her heart and her own breathing. The subtle scent of his after-shave permeated the air and mingled with her perfume.

Mark sighed and turned to her. "Kaite, I've been

driving around trying to find the right words to tell you I'm sorry. I've acted like a real Dumbo. I don't know why I ever believed there was anything going on between you and Pete Milton. I should have known you wouldn't go for a jerk like that and I just want to say I'm sorry and—and I guess I said that.'' He paused and shook his head. ''I kind of wondered—I wondered if—well, if you'd like to go to the beach tomorrow?'' Mark sounded breathless, as if he'd just run an extra long race.

''The beach sounds great,'' Kaite said, surprised at how together she sounded, when her insides were doing enormous flip-flops. She wanted to put her arms around him and tell him that her feelings for him hadn't changed one bit.

''You will? You aren't mad?''

''I was hurt, Mark. I thought we were at least friends and that we could talk, but you wouldn't listen to me. You didn't even return my phone calls.''

Mark took her hand. He stroked her fingers with his thumb. ''I know. My parents tell me all the time how pigheaded I am. I'll try to make it up to you. Please, Kaite, give me another chance. Can we start over?''

Kaite glanced toward the house. ''I guess you've given me plenty of other chances, considering what my brothers and sisters seem to put you through each time you're here.''

''That's not your fault, and it's not the same thing at all. I really like your family. There's always a surprise when I'm here. Nothing's predictable, the way it is at my house.''

Kaite shook her head. She couldn't believe that Mark actually liked all the pranks that her brothers and sisters played on them. But she didn't really want them or him any other way. If you liked one Grover, you were stuck with liking the rest. She smiled softly, thinking that maybe she should have invited Pete over a few times. Maybe she'd gone about discouraging him the wrong way.

"What's so funny?" Mark asked.

"Nothing's funny. Everything is wonderful," said Kaite.

"For me, too." Mark put his arms around her and pulled her toward him. She rested her head on his chest. He slipped his hand under her chin and tilted her head so she looked into his eyes. Then he bent his head and his lips were soft and warm on her own. "You're a special girl, Kaite," he whispered, "and I love you."

Their lips met again in a kiss that left both of them breathless.

"I'd better go in," Kaite said as her heart raced with excitement and happiness.

"I'll walk you to the door." He hugged her before getting out of the car.

Mark held Kaite's hand tightly in his as they went up the front walk. On the porch he turned her to face him. They stood, arms around each other, just smiling. She wanted to memorize his face, to stamp everything about these past few minutes in her mind forever. Kaite rested her head against his chest and listened to the reassuring beat of his heart. She wanted to stay like that forever, secure in Mark's arms, certain that he loved her.

"Can you see them?" A whisper came from somewhere above them.

Kaite looked up. "Oh, no," she whispered.

Mark's body started to shake as he suppressed a laugh. "Listen," he said softly.

"Are they kissing yet?" A few giggles.

"I can't see anything."

"I want to look, too."

Kaite tried to see where the kids were. "They should all be sound asleep."

Mark grinned. "One of them must have seen my car in front. As usual, it's just me, you, and the zoo," he said softly, pulling her close to kiss her once more.

Kaite was vaguely aware of giggles. "Now," said one of her brothers.

As Mark pulled away from her, a long strip of toilet paper fluttered down from the upstairs bathroom window. Mark grabbed it. In smeared marking pen letters, Kaite could just make out the words: HI, MARK.

Mark started to laugh and so did Kaite. "Tell them I'll see them tomorrow. Maybe they'd like to go with us?"

"Uh-uh," said Kaite. "Tomorrow it's just me and you. The zoo stays home."

"I know what. I'll bring Chaos to visit. But you'd better warn your mother."

"I'm sure she won't mind much. What's a little more chaos in the Grover family?"

Mark laughed and hugged her. "Until tomorrow," he said, then walked down the front walk.

Kaite watched until his car was gone. She tugged at the strip of paper, rolled it up, and went inside. She closed the door firmly, so that the sound echoed through the house. Then she started up the stairs with definite steps.

A chorus of giggles and the patter of feet sounded in the upstairs hall as the zoo escaped to their beds.

"Ready or not," she called, "here I come."

Now that you're reading the best in teen romance, why not make that *Caprice* feeling part of your own special look? Four great gifts to accent that "unique something" in you are all yours when you collect the proof-of-purchase from the back of any current *Caprice* romance!

Each proof-of-purchase is worth 3 Heart Points toward these items available <u>only</u> from *Caprice*. And what better way to make them yours than by reading the romances every teen is talking about! Start collecting today!

Proof-of-purchase is worth 3 Heart Points toward one of four exciting premiums bearing the distinctive *Caprice* logo

CAPRICE PREMIUMS
Berkley Publishing Group, Inc./Dept. LB
200 Madison Avenue, New York, NY 10016

PROOF OF PURCHASE
—3—
HEART POINTS
DETAILS INSIDE

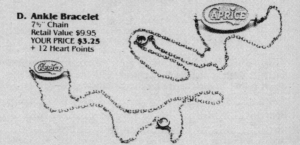